幸福

〔英〕曼殊斐尔／著

徐志摩／译

曼殊斐尔小说集

时代文艺出版社

图书在版编目（CIP）数据

幸福：曼殊斐尔小说集 /（英）曼殊斐尔 著；徐志摩 译.
—长春：时代文艺出版社，2012.7（2021.5重印）

ISBN 978-7-5387-4085-1

I. ①幸... II. ①曼...②徐... III. ①短篇小说－小说集－英国－现代 IV. ①I561.45

中国版本图书馆CIP数据核字（2012）第143323号

出品人	陈　琛
责任编辑	付　娜
装帧设计	孙　俪
排版制作	隋淑凤

幸福：曼殊斐尔小说集

[英] 曼殊斐尔 著　徐志摩 译

出版发行 / 时代文艺出版社
地址 / 长春市福祉大路5788号　龙腾国际大厦A座15层　邮编 / 130118
总编办 / 0431-81629751　发行部 / 0431-81629755
官方微博 / weibo.com / tlapress　天猫旗舰店 / sdwycbsgf.tmall.com
印刷 / 保定市铭泰达印刷有限公司
开本 / 640×980毫米　1 / 20　字数 / 134千字　印张 / 12
版次 / 2012年9月第1版　印次 / 2021年5月第2次印刷　定价 / 39.80元

出版说明

　　本书是由英国作家曼殊斐尔创作的短篇小说选集。曼殊斐尔（Katherine Mansfield），通译为凯瑟琳·曼斯菲尔德（1888～1923），英国著名的女作家。生于新西兰的惠灵顿，年轻时到伦敦求学，后在英国定居。她是以短篇小说成名的，在作品风格上，富有女性的特点，细腻而干净，笔调自然流畅，在技巧方面注重心理描写，综合了多种现代主义的表现方法，这使她的作品在西方国家颇受欢迎，也在20世纪20年代得到了东方青年读者的广泛阅读。

　　曼殊斐尔于1922年7月，在伦敦会见徐志摩，交谈中她给徐志摩留下深刻的印象，虽然只有20分钟的会面，却使徐志摩受到了一次美的洗礼，并和其结下了终生的深厚友谊。所以在和曼殊斐尔见面时，徐志摩接受了翻译她小说的重托，当年10月15日，徐志摩从英国返回中国。归国后，他没有食言，在多次讲演或撰文介绍这位令他动心的女作家之余，他翻译成了《曼殊斐尔小说集》，为曼殊斐尔的作品在中国的流布立下了筚路蓝缕之功。曼殊斐尔因患有肺结核病，于1923年1月9日在法国的枫丹白露镇去世。

徐志摩一生顶礼膜拜的女性美的理想，只和他接触了20分钟，"那二十分钟不死的时间"成为徐志摩终生的眷恋。在得知曼殊斐尔逝世之后，徐志摩一腔哀思难平，写下诗歌《哀曼殊斐尔》(《努力周报》第44期)。在回忆文章《曼殊斐尔》中，徐志摩用"感美感恋最纯粹的一俄顷之回忆"来表达自己对曼殊斐尔的深情怀念。曼殊斐尔逝世半年之后，徐志摩还赶到巴黎曼殊斐尔的墓地凭吊，"怅望云天，泪下点点"。

徐志摩译著的《曼殊斐尔小说集》，于1927年由北新书局初版中文繁体毛边本。此次出版是1927年初版之后的国内首次简体中文出版，不仅收有精心挑选的曼殊斐尔的几个短篇小说，还特别收录了徐志摩为哀悼曼殊斐尔而写的纪念文章《曼殊斐尔》和诗歌《哀曼殊斐尔》。而且，本书首次采用了中文、英语的双语版本，以满足读者的不同阅读口味，为读者尽心呈现绝美的阅读和视觉的盛宴。

目 录
CONTENTS

哀曼殊斐尔

徐志摩

我昨夜梦入幽谷，

听子规在百合丛中泣血，

我昨夜梦登高峰，

见一颗光明泪自天坠落。

罗马西郊有座暮园，

芝罗兰静掩着客殇的诗骸；

百年后海岱士^①（Hades）黑辇之轮。

又喧响于芳丹卜罗^②榆青之间。

----

① 原文为"海岱士"（Hades），现通译为"哈得斯"，希腊神话中的冥王。为了让读者能欣赏到徐志摩诗歌的原汁原味，此处仍保留徐志摩的译法。——编者注

② 原文为"芳丹卜罗"，现通译为"枫丹白露"，法国著名的风景区。为了让读者能欣赏到徐志摩诗歌的原汁原味，此处仍保留徐志摩的译法。——编者注

说宇宙是无情的机械，

为甚明灯似的理想闪耀在前；

说造化是真善美之创现，

为甚五彩虹不常住天边？

我与你虽仅一度相见——

但那二十分不死的时间！

谁能信你那仙姿灵态，

竟已朝露似的永别人间？

非也！生命只是个实体的幻梦；

美丽的灵魂，永承上帝的爱宠；

三十年小住，只似昙花之偶现，

泪花里我想见你笑归仙宫。

你记否伦敦约言，曼殊斐尔！

今夏再见于琴妮湖① (Lake Geneva) 之边；

琴妮湖永抱着白朗矶的雪影，

此日我怅望云天，泪下点点！

---

① 原文为"琴妮湖"（Lake Geneva），现通译为"日内瓦湖"。为了让读者能欣赏到徐志摩诗歌的原汁原味，此处仍保留徐志摩的译法。——编者注

我当年初临生命的消息，
梦觉似的骤感恋爱之庄严；
生命的觉悟是爱之成年，
我今又因死而感生与恋之涯沿！

因情是掼不破的纯晶，
爱是实现生命之唯一途径：
死是座伟秘的洪炉，此中
凝炼万象所从来之神明。

我哀思焉能电花似的飞聘，
感动你在天日遥远的灵魂？
我洒泪向风中遥送，
问何时能戡破生死之门？

一九二三年三月十一日作

园　会

The Garden Party

那天的天气果然是理想的。园会的天气，就是他们预定的，也没有再好的了。没有风，暖和，天上没有云点子。就是蓝天里盖着一层淡金色的雾纱，像是初夏有时的天气。那园丁天亮就起来，剪草，扫地，收拾个干净；草地和那种着小菊花的暗暗的平顶的小花房儿，都闪闪地发亮着。还有那些玫瑰花，她们自个儿真像是懂得，到园会的人们也就只会得赏识玫瑰花儿；这是谁都认得的花儿。好几百，真是好几百，全在一夜里开了出来；那一丛绿绿的全低着头儿，像是天仙来拜会过他们似的。

他们早餐还没有吃完，工人们就来安那布篷子。

"娘，你看这篷子安在哪儿好？"

"我的好孩子，用不着问我。今年我是打定主意什么事都交给你们孩子们的了。忘了我是你们的娘。只当我是个请来的贵客就得。"

但是梅格总还不能去监督那些工人们。她没有吃早饭就洗了头发，她带着一块青的头巾坐在那里喝咖啡，潮的黑的发鬓儿贴在她两边的脸上。乔斯①，那蝴蝶儿，每天下来总是穿着绸的里裙，披着日本的花衫子。

"还是你去吧，劳拉②，你是讲究美术的。"

---

①② 为了更加符合现代读者的阅读习惯，本书将原书中民国时期的英文译名"玖思"(Jose) 改为现今通行的译名"乔斯"；"老腊"(Laura) 改为"劳拉"。——编者注

劳拉就飞了出去，手里还拿着她的一块牛油面包。

　　她就爱有了推头到屋子外面吃东西；她又是最爱安排事情的；她总以为她可以比谁都办得稳当些。

　　四个工人，脱了外褂子的，一块儿站在园里的道儿上。他们手里拿着支篷帐的杆子，一卷卷的帆布，背上挂着装工具的大口袋儿。他们的神气很叫人注意的。劳拉现在倒怪怨她还拿着那片牛油面包，可是又没有地方放，她又不能把它掷了。她脸上有点儿红，她走近他们的时候；可是她装出严厉的，甚至有点儿近视的样子。

　　"早安，"她说，学她娘的口气。但是这一声装得太可怕了，她自己都有点儿难为情，接着她就像个小女孩子口吃着说，"啊——欧——你们来——是不是为那篷帐？"

　　"就是您哪，小姐，"身子最高的那个说，一个瘦瘦的，满脸斑点的高个儿，他掀动着他背上的大口袋，把他的草帽往后脑一推，望下来对着她笑，"就是为那个。"

　　他的笑那样的随便，那样的和气，劳拉也就不觉得难为情了。多么好的眼他有的是，小小的，可是那样的深蓝！她现在望着他的同伴，他们也在笑吟吟的。"放心，我们不咬人的，"他们的笑像在那儿说。工人们多么好呀！这早上又是多美呀！可是她不该提起早上，她得办她的公事。那篷帐。

"我说，把他放在那边百合花的草地上，怎么样呢？那边成不成？"

她伸着不拿牛油面包的那只手，点着那百合花的草地。他们转过身去，望着她点的方向。那小胖子扁着他那下嘴唇皮儿，那高个子皱着眉头。

"我瞧不合适，"他说，"看得不够明亮。您瞧，要是一个漫天帐子，"他转身向着劳拉，还是他那随便的样子，"您得放着一个地基儿，您一看就会嘭地一下打着你的眼，要是您懂我的话。"

这一下可是把劳拉蒙住了一阵子，她想不清一个做工的该不该对她说那样的话，嘭地一下打着你的眼。她可是很懂得。

"那边网球场的一个基角儿上呢？"她又出主意。"可是音乐队也得占一个基角儿。"

"唔，还有音乐队不是？"又一个工人说。他的脸是青青的。他的眼睛瞄着那网球场，神情怪难看的，他在想什么呢？

"就是一个很小的音乐队。"劳拉缓缓地说。也许他不会多么的介意，要是音乐队是个小的。但是那高个儿的又打岔了。

"我说，小姐，那个地基儿合适，背着前面那些大树。那边儿，准合适。"

背那些喀拉噶树。可是那些喀拉噶树得被遮住了。他们多么可爱，宽宽的，发亮的叶子，一球球的黄果子。他们像是你想象长在一个荒岛上的大树，高傲的，孤单的，对着太阳擎着他们的叶子，果子，冷静壮丽的神气。他们免不了让那篷帐遮住吗？

免不了。工人们已经扛起他们的杆子，向着那个地基儿去了。就是那高个儿的还没有走。他弯下身子去，捻着一小枝的薰衣草①，把他的大拇指与食指放在鼻子边，嗅吸了沾着的香气。劳拉看了他那手势，把什么喀拉噶树全忘了，她就不懂得一个做工人会注意到那些个东西——爱薰衣草的味儿。她认识的能有几个人会做这样的事。做工人多么异常的有意思呀，她心里想。为什么她就不能跟做工人做朋友，强如那些粗蠢的男孩子们，伴她跳舞的，星期日晚上来吃夜饭的？他们准是合适得多。

坏处就在，她心里打算，一面那高个的工人正在一个信封的后背画什么东西，错处就在那些个可笑的阶级区别，枪毙或是绞死了那一点子就没有事儿了。就她自个儿说呢，她简直想不着什么区别不区别。一点儿，一子儿都没有……现在木槌子打桩的声音已经来了。有人在那儿嘘口调子，有人唱了出来，"你那儿合适不合适，玛代？""玛代！"那要好的意思，那——那——她想表示她多么的快活，让那高个儿的明白她多么的随便，她多么的瞧不起蠢笨的习惯，劳拉就拿起她手里的牛油面包来，使劲地啃了一大口，一面瞪着眼看她的小画。她觉得她真是个做工的女

---

① 为了更加符合现代读者的阅读习惯，本书将原书中民国时期的英文译名"拉芬特草"（Lavender）改为现今通行的译名"薰衣草"。——编者注

孩子似的。

"劳拉，劳拉，你在哪儿？有电话，劳拉！"一个声音从屋子里叫了出来。

"来——了！"她就燕子似的掠了去，穿草地，上道儿，上阶沿儿，穿走廊子，进门儿，在前厅里她的爹与劳里①正在刷他们的帽子，预备办事去。

"我说，劳拉，"劳里快快地说，"下半天以前你替我看看我的褂子，成不成？看看要收拾不要。""算数。"她说。忽然她自个儿忍不住了。她跑到劳里身边，把他小小地，快快地挤了一下。"啊，我真爱茶会呀，你爱不爱？"劳拉喘着气说。

"可——不是，"劳里用亲密的、孩子的口音说，他也拿他的妹妹挤了一下，把她轻轻地一推，"忙你的电话去，小姐。"

那电话。"对的，对的；对呀。基蒂②？早安，我的乖。来吃中饭？一定来，我的乖。当然好极了。没有东西，就是顶随便的便饭——就是面包壳儿，碎蛋白糖饼壳儿，还有昨天剩下来的什么。是，这早上天气真好不是？等一等——别挂。娘在叫哪。"劳拉坐了下来。

"什么，娘？听不着。"

---

①② 为了更加符合现代读者的阅读习惯，本书将原书中民国时期的英文译名"老利"(Laurie) 改为现今通行的"劳里"；"开弟" (Kitty) 改为"基蒂"。——编者注

谢里登^①太太的声音从楼梯上飘了下来："告诉她还是戴她上礼拜天戴的那顶漂亮帽子。"

"娘说你还是戴你上礼拜天戴的那顶漂亮帽子，好。一点钟，再会。"

劳拉放回了听筒，手臂往脑袋背后一甩，深深地呼了一口气，伸了一个懒腰，手臂又落了下来。"呼"，她叹了口气，快快地重复坐正了。她是静静的，听着。屋子里所有的门户像是全打得大开似的。满屋子只是轻的、快的脚步声，流动的口音。那扇绿布包着的门，通厨房那一带去的，不住地摆着，塞，塞地响。一会儿又听着一个长长的，气呼呼的怪响。那是他们在移动那笨重的钢琴，圆转脚儿擦着地板的声音。但是那空气！要是你静着听，难道那空气总是这样的？小小的，软弱的风在闹着玩儿，一会儿往着窗格子顶上冲了进来，一会儿带了门儿跑了出去。还有两小点儿的阳光也在那儿闹着玩，一点在墨水瓶上，一点在白银的照相架上。乖乖的小点子。尤其是在墨水瓶盖上的那一点。看的顶亲热的。一个小小的、热热的银星儿。她去亲吻他都成。

前门的小铃子丁丁地响了，接着萨迪^②印花布裙子窸窣地上

楼梯。一个男子的口音在含糊地说话，萨迪答话，不使劲地："我不知道呀。等着。我来问问谢里登太太。"

"什么事，萨迪？"劳拉走进了前厅。

"为那卖花的，劳拉小姐。"

不错，是的。那边，靠近门儿，一个宽大的浅盘子，里面满放着一盆盆的粉红百合花儿。就是一种花。就是百合——美人蕉①，大的红的花朵儿，开得满满的，亮亮的，在鲜艳的、深红色花梗子上长着，简直像有灵性的一样。

"啊——啊，萨迪！"劳拉说，带着小小的哭声似的。她蹲了下去，像是到百合花的光焰里去取暖似的；她觉着他们是在她的手指上，在她的口唇上，在她的心窝里长着。

"错了，"她软音地说。"我们没有定要这么多的。萨迪，去问娘去。"

但是正在这个当儿谢里登太太也过来了。

"不错的"，她静静地说。"是我定要的。这花儿多么可爱？"她挤紧着劳拉的臂膀。"昨天我走过那家花铺子，我在窗子里看着了。我想我这一次总要买他一个痛快。园会不是一个很好的推头吗？"

---

① 为了更加符合现代读者的阅读习惯，本书将原书中民国时期的英文译名"肯那百合"（canna lily）改为现今通行的译名"美人蕉"。——编者注

"可是我以为你说过你不来管我们的事。"劳拉说。萨迪已经走开了，送花来的小工还靠近他的手车站在门外。她伸出手臂去绕着她娘的项颈，轻轻的，很轻轻的，她咬着他娘的耳朵。

"我的乖孩子，你也不愿意有一个过分刻板的娘不是？别孩子气。挑花的又来了。"

他又拿进了很多的百合花，满满的又是一大盘儿。"一条边地放着，就在进门那儿，门框子的两面，劳驾"，谢里登太太说。"你看好不好，劳拉？"

"好，真好，娘。"

在那客厅里，梅格，乔斯，还有那好的小汉斯，三个人好容易把那钢琴移好了。

"我说，把这柜子靠着墙，屋子里什么都搬走，除了椅子，你们看怎么样？"

"成。"

"汉斯，把这几个桌子搬到休息室里去，拿一把帚子进来把地毯上的桌腿子痕子扫了——等一等，汉斯——"乔斯就爱吩咐底下人，他们也爱听她。她那神气就像他们一块儿在唱戏似的。"要太太、劳拉小姐就上这儿来。"

"就是，乔斯小姐。"

她又转身对梅格说话："我要听听那琴今天成不成，回头下半天他们也许要我唱。我们来试试那'This life is weary'。"

嘭！他！他，氏！他！那琴声突然很热烈地响了出来，乔斯的面色都变了。她握紧了自己的手。她娘同劳拉刚进来，她对她们望着。一脸的忧郁，一脸的奥妙。

　　　　这样的生活是疲——倦的，
　　　　一滴眼泪，一声叹气。
　　　　爱情也是要变——心的
　　　　这样的生活是疲——倦的，
　　　　一滴眼泪，一声叹气。
　　　　爱情也是不久——长的，
　　　　时候到了……再见！

但是她唱到"再见"的时候，虽则琴声格外地绝望了，她的脸上忽然泛出鲜明的、异常地不同情的笑容。

"我的嗓子成不成，妈妈？"她脸上亮着。

　　　　这样的生活是疲——倦的，
　　　　希望来了，还是要死的。
　　　　一场梦境，一场惊醒。

但是现在萨迪打断了她们。"什么事，萨迪？"

"说是，太太，厨娘说面包饼上的小纸旗儿有没有？"

"面包饼上的小纸旗儿，萨迪？"谢里登太太在梦里似的回应着。那些小孩子一看她的脸就知道她没有小旗儿。

"我想想。"一会儿，她对萨迪坚定地说，"告诉那厨娘等十分钟我就给她。"

萨迪去了。

"我说，劳拉"，她母亲快快地说，"跟我到休息间里来。旗子的几个名字我写在一张信封的后背。你来替我写了出来。梅格，马上上楼去，把你头上那湿东西去了。乔斯，你也马上去把衣服穿好了。听着了没有，孩子们，要不然回头你们爹晚上回家的时候我告诉他？说是——乔斯，你要到厨房里去，告诉那厨娘别着急，好不好？这早上我怕死了她。"

那张信封好容易在饭间里那摆钟背后找了出来。怎么会在那儿，谢里登太太想都想不着了。

"定是你们里面不知谁从我的手袋里偷了出来，我记得顶清楚的——奶酪起司同柠檬奶冻。写下了没有？"

"写了。"

"鸡子同——"，谢里登太太把那张信封擎得远远的。"什么字，看着像是小老鼠。不会是小老鼠。不是？"

"青果，宝贝。"劳拉说，回过头来望着。

"可不是，青果，对的。这两样东西并着念多怪呀。鸡子同青果。"

她们好容易把那几张旗子写完。劳拉就拿走到厨房去了。她见乔斯正在那里平厨娘的着急，那厨娘可是一点儿也不怕人。

"我从没有见过这样精巧的面包饼，"乔斯乐疯了的口音说。"你说这儿一共有几种，厨娘？十五对不对？"

"十五，乔斯小姐。"

"好，厨娘，我恭喜你。"

厨娘手里拿着切面包饼的长刀，抹下了桌上的碎粉屑儿，开了一张嘴尽笑。

"戈德伯①铺子里的来了。"萨迪喊着，从伙食房里走出来。她看见那人在窗子外面走过。

这就是说奶油松饼来了。高德伯那家店铺，就是做奶油松饼出名。有了他们的，谁都不愿意自己在家里做。

"去拿进来放在桌子上吧，姑娘。"厨娘吩咐。

萨迪去拿了进来，又去了。劳拉与乔斯当然是长大了，不会认真的见了奶油什么就上劲。可是她们也就忍不住同声地赞美，

----

① 为了更加符合现代读者的阅读习惯，本书将原书中民国时期的英文译名"高德"（Godber）改为现今通行的译名"戈德伯"。——编者注

说这松饼做得真可爱呀。太美了。厨娘动手拾掇，摇下了多余的糖冰。

"一见这些个松饼儿，像是你一辈子的茶会全回来了似的，你说是不是？"劳拉说。

"许有的事，"讲究实际的乔斯说，她从不想回到从前去的，"他们看起来这样美丽轻巧，羽毛似的，我说。"

"一人拿一个吧，我的乖乖，"厨娘说，她那快乐的口音。"你的妈不会知道的。"

这哪儿成。想想，才吃早饭，就吃奶油松饼。一想着都叫人难受。可是要不了两分钟，乔斯与劳拉都在舔她们的手指儿了，她们那得意的，心里快活的神气，一看就知道她们是才吃了新鲜奶油的。

"我们到园里去，从后门出去，"劳拉出主意。"我要去看看工人们的篷帐怎么样了。那工人们真有意思。"

但是后门的道儿，让厨娘、萨迪、高德伯铺子里的伙计、小汉斯几个人拦住了。

出了事了。

"格——格——格"，厨娘咯咯地叫着，像一只吓慌了的母鸡。萨迪的一只手抓紧了她的下巴，像是牙痛似的。小汉斯的脸子像螺旋似的邹着，摸不着头脑。就是高德伯铺子里来的伙计看是自己儿得意似的，这故事是他讲的。

"什么事？出了什么事？"

"出了大乱子了，"厨娘说，"一个男子死了。"

"一个男子死了！哪儿？怎么的？什么时候？"

但是那店伙计可不愿意现鲜鲜的新闻，让人家当着他面抢着讲。

"知道那些个小屋子就在这儿下去的，小姐？"知道？当然她知道。"得，有个年轻的住在那儿，名字叫斯科特①，赶大车儿的。他的马见了那平道儿的机器，今天早上在霍克路的基角儿上，他那马见了就发傻，一个跟斗就把他掷了下去，掷在他脑袋的后背。死了。"

"死了！"劳拉瞪着眼望着那伙计。

"他们把他捡起来的时候就死了，"那伙计讲得更起劲了。"我来的时候正碰着他们把那尸体抬回家去。"他对着厨娘说，"他剩下一个妻子，五个小的。"

"乔斯，这儿来。"她一把拉住了她妹子的衣袖，牵着她穿过了厨房，到绿布门的那一面。她停下了，靠在门边。"乔斯！"她说，吓坏了的，"这怎么办，我们有什么法子把什么事

① 为了更加符合现代读者的阅读习惯，本书将原书中民国时期的英文译名"司考脱"（Scott）改为现今通行的译名"斯科特"。——编者注

都停了呢？"

"什么事都停了，劳拉！"乔斯骇然地说。"这怎么讲？"

"把园会停了，当然。"乔斯为什么要装假？

但是乔斯反而更糊涂了。"把园会停了？劳拉我的乖，别那么傻。当然我们不干这样的事，也没有人想我们这么办。别太过分了。"

"可是现鲜鲜的有人死在我们的大门外，我们怎么能举行园会呢？"

这话实在是太过分了，因为那些小屋子有他们自个儿的一条小巷，在她们家一直斜下去的那条街的尽头。中间还隔着一条顶宽的大路哪。不错，他们是太贴近一点。那些小屋子看得真让人眼痛，他们就不应该在这一带的附近。就是几间小小的烂房子，画成朱古力棕褐色的。他们的背后园里也就是菜梗子，瘦小的母鸡子，红茄的罐子。他们烟囱里冒出来的烟，先就是寒碜。烂布似的，烂片似的小烟卷儿，哪儿比得上谢里登家的烟囱里出来的，那样大片的，银色的羽毛，在天空里荡着。洗衣服的妇人们住在那条小巷里，还有扫烟囱的，一个补鞋的，还有一个男的，他的门前满挂着小雀笼子。孩子们又是成群的。谢里登家的孩子小的时候，他们是一步也不准上那儿去的，怕的是他们学下流话，沾染他们下流的脾气。但是自从他们长成了，劳拉同劳里有时也穿着那道儿走。又肮脏，又讨厌。他们走过都觉得难受。可是一个人什么地方都得去，什么事情都得亲眼看。他们就是这样地走过了。

"你只要想想我们的音乐队一动手，叫那苦恼的妇人怎么受得住！"劳拉说。

"啊，劳拉！"乔斯现在认真的着恼了。"要是每次有人碰着了意外，你的音乐队就得停起来，你的一辈子也就够受了。我也是和你一样的难过。我也是一样的软心肠的。"她的眼睛发狠了。她那盯着她的姊姊的神气，就像是她们小时候打架的样子。"你这样的感情作用也救不活一个做工的酒鬼。"她软软地说。

"酒鬼！谁说他是酒醉！"劳拉也发狠地对着乔斯。"我马上就进去告诉娘去。"她说，正像她从前每次闹翻了说的话。

"请，我的乖。"乔斯甜着口音说。

"娘呀，我可以到你的房里吗？"劳拉手持着那大的玻璃门拳儿。

"来吧，孩子。唉，怎么回事？怎么你的脸上红红的？"谢里登太太从她的镜台边转了过来。她正在试她的新帽子。

"娘，有一个人摔死了。"劳拉开头说。

"不是在我们的园里？"她娘就打岔。

"不，不！"

"啊，你真是吓了我一跳。"谢里登太太叹了口气，放心了，拿下了她的大帽子，放在她的膝腿上。

"可是你听我说，娘，"劳拉说。她把这可怕的故事讲了，气都喘不过来。"当然，我们不能开茶会了不是，"她恳求地说。"音乐队，什么人都快到了。他们听得到的，娘；他们差不多是近邻！"

她娘的态度竟是同乔斯方才一样，劳拉真骇然了！更难受的是因为她看是好玩似的。她竟没有把劳拉认真对待。

"但是，我的好孩子，你得应用你的常识。这无非是偶然的，我们听着了那回事。要是那边有人生病了——我就不懂得他们挤在那些脏死的小窠儿里，怎么的活法——我们还不是一样地开我们的茶会不是？"

劳拉只好回答说"是的"，可是她心里想这是全错的。她在她娘的沙发椅上坐了下来，捻着那椅垫的绉边。

"娘，这不是我们真的连一点慈悲心都没有了吗？"

"乖孩子！"谢里登太太站起身走过来了，拿着那帽子。劳拉来不及拦阻，她已经把那帽子套在她的头上。"我的孩子！"她娘说，"这帽子是你的。天生是你的。这帽子我戴太嫌年轻了，我从没有见过你这样的一张画似的。你自己看看。"她就拿着手镜要她看。

"可是，娘，"劳拉又起了一个头。她不能看她自己；她把身子转了过去。

这一来谢里登太太可也忍不住了，就像方才乔斯忍不住了一样。

"你这是太离奇了，劳拉，"她冷冷地说。"像他们那样的人家也不想我们牺牲什么。况且像你这样要什么人都不乐意，也不见怎样的发善心不是？"

"我不懂。"劳拉说，她快快地走了出去，进了她自己的卧房。在那里，很是无意的，她最先见着的，就是镜子里的一个可爱的姑娘，戴着她那黑帽子金小花儿装边的，还有一条长的黑丝绒带子。她从没想过她能有这样的好看。娘是对的吗？她想。现在她竟是希望娘是对的。我不是太过分吗？许是太过分了。就是一转瞬间，她又见着了那可怜的妇人同她的小孩子，她男人的尸体抬到屋子里去。但这都是模糊的，不真切的，像新闻纸上的图画似的。等茶会过了我再想着吧，她定主意了。这像是最妥当的办法了……

中饭吃过一点半。两点半的时候他们已经准备这场闹了。穿绿褂子的音乐队已经到了，在那网球场的犄角儿上落坐了。

"我的乖！"基蒂·梅特兰娇音地说，"可不是他们太像青虾蟆？你们应该让他们围着那小池子蹲着，让那领班的站在池中间一张花叶子上。"

劳里也到了，一路招呼着进去换衣服了。一见着他，劳拉又想起那件祸事了。她要告诉他。如其劳里也同其余的见解一样，这就不用说一定是不错的了。她跟着他进了前厅。

"劳里！"

"哎！"他已经是半扶梯，但是他转身来见了劳拉，他就鼓起了他的腮帮子，睁着大眼睛望着她。"我说，劳拉！你叫我眼都看花了，"劳里说，"多，多漂亮的帽子！"

劳拉轻轻地说："真的吗？"她仰着头对劳里笑着，到底还是没有告诉他。

不多一会见客人像潮水一般来了。音乐队动手了，雇来的听差忙着从屋子跑到篷帐里去。随你向哪儿望，总有一对对的在缓缓地走着，弯着身子看花，打招呼，在草地上过去。客人们像是美丽的鸟雀儿，在这下半天停在谢里登家的园子里，顺路到——哪儿呢？啊，多快活呀，碰着的全是快活人，握着手，贴着脸子，对着眼睛笑。

"劳拉乖乖，你多美呀！"

"你的帽子多合适呀，孩子！"

"劳拉，你样子顶像西班牙美人，我从没有见你这样漂亮过。"

劳拉抖擞着，也就软软地回答："你喝了茶没有？来点儿冰吧；今天的果子冰倒真是别致的。"她跑到她爹那里去，求着他，"好爹爹，音乐队让他们喝点儿水吧？"

这圆满的下午渐渐地成熟了，渐渐地衰谢了，渐渐地花瓣儿全闭着了。

"再没有更满意的园会……""大，大成功……""真要算是最，最……"

劳拉帮着她娘说再会。她们一并肩地站在门口，一直等到完事。

"完了，完了，谢谢天，"谢里登太太说。"把他们全找来，劳拉。我们去喝一点新鲜咖啡去。我累坏了。总算是很成功的。可是这些茶会，这些茶会！为什么你们一定不放过要开茶会！"他们全在走空了的篷帐里坐了下来。

"来一块面包夹饼，爹爹。旗子是我写的。"

"多谢。"谢里登先生咬了一口，那块饼就不见了。他又吃了一块。"我想你们没有听见今天出的骇人的乱子吗？"

"我的乖，"谢里登太太说，举着她的一只手，"我们听见的。险一点把我们的茶会都弄糟了。劳拉硬主张我们把会停了。"

"啊，娘呀！"劳拉不愿意为这件事再受嘲讽。

"总是一件可怕的事情不是？"谢里登先生说。"那死的也成了家了。就住在这儿下去那个小巷子里，他抛下了一个妻子，半打小孩，他们说。"

很不自然地小静了一会。太太的手不安地弄着她的茶杯。实在爹不识趣了……

忽然她仰起头来望着。桌子上满是那些个面包夹饼、蛋糕、奶饼油松，全没有吃，回头全是没有用的。她想着了她的一个妙主意。

"我知道了，"她说。"我们装起一个篮子来吧。我们拿点儿这完全没有动的上好点心，给那可怜的女人吧。随便怎么样，她的小孩子们总有了一顿大大的食品，你们说对不对？并且她总有邻舍人等出出进进的。不劳她费心这全是现成的，可不是个好主意？"

"劳拉！"说着她跳了起来，"把那楼梯边柜子里的那大竹篮子拿来。"

"但是，娘，你难道真以为这是个好主意吗？"劳拉说。

又是一次，多奇怪，她的见解与旁人不同了。拿她们茶会余下的滓子去给人家。那可怜的妇人真的就会乐意吗？

"当然啰！今天你怎么的？方才不多一会儿，你抱怨着人家不发慈悲，可是现在——"

啊，好的！劳拉跑去把篮子拿来了。装满了，堆满了，她娘自己动手的。

"你自己拿了去，乖乖，"她说，"你就是这样去好了。不，等一等，也带一点大红花去。他们那一等人顶喜欢这大花儿的。"

"小心那花梗子毁了她的新花边衣。"讲究实际的乔斯说。

真会的。还好，来得及。"那你就拿这竹篮子吧。喂，劳拉！"她娘跟她出了篷帐——"随便怎样你可不要——"

"什么，娘？"

不，这种意思还是不装进孩子的脑袋里去好！"没有事！你跑吧！"

劳拉关上园门的时候，天已经快黄昏了。一只大狗像一个黑影子似的跑过。这道儿白白的亮着，望下去那块凹地里暗沉沉的就是那些小屋子。

过了那半天的热闹这时候多静呀。她现在独自走下那斜坡去，到一个地方，那里说是有个男子死了，她可是有点儿想不清似的。为什么她想不清？她停步了一会儿。她的内心像满蒙着亲吻呀，种种的口音呀，杯匙丁当的响声呀，笑呀，压平的青草味呀，塞得满满的。她再没有余地，放别的东西。多怪呀！她仰起头望着苍白的天，她心里想着的就是："对呀，这真是顶满意的茶会。"

现在那条大路已经走过了。已经近了那小巷，烟沉沉的、黑沉沉的。披着围巾的女人，戴着粗便帽的男人匆忙地走着。有的男人靠在木棚子上；小孩子们在门前玩着。一阵低低的嗡嗡的声响，从那卑污的小屋子里出来。有的屋子里有一星的灯亮，一个黑影子，螃蟹似的，在窗子里移动着。劳拉低了头快快地走。她现在倒抱怨没有裹上一件外衣出来。她的上身衣闪得多亮呀！还有那黑丝绒飘带的大帽子——换一顶帽子多好！人家不是望着她吗？他们一定在望着她。这一来来错了；她早知道错了。她现在再回去怎么样呢？

不，太迟了。这就是那家人家。一定是的，暗暗的一堆人站在外面。门边一张椅子里坐着一个很老的老婆子，手里拿着一根拐杖，她在看热闹，她的一双脚踏在一张报纸上。劳拉一走近人声就停了。这群人也散了。倒像是他们知道她要到这儿来似的，像是他们在等着她哪。

劳拉异常地不自在。颠着她肩上的丝绒带子，她问一个站在旁边的妇人："这是斯科特夫人的家吗？"那个妇人，古怪地笑着，回说："这是的，小姑娘。"

啊，这情形躲得了多好！她走上他们门前的走道，伸手敲门的时候，她真的说了："帮助我，上帝。"只要躲得了他们那弹出的眼睛，这是有什么法子把自己裹了起来，裹在一个围肩里都好。我放下了这篮子就走，她打定了主意。我连空篮子都不等了。

那门开了。一个穿黑的小女人在暗冥里替她开着门。

劳拉说："你是斯科特夫人吗？"但是那女人的答话吓了劳拉一跳："请进来吧，小姐。"她让她关进在门里了。

"不，"劳拉说，"我不进去了。我只是要放下这篮子。娘叫我送来——"

在黑沉沉的夹道儿里的小女人像是没有听着似的。"走这儿，请，小姐。"她软媚的口音说，劳拉跟了进去。

她进了一间破烂的，又低又窄的厨房，台上一盏冒烟的油灯。灶火的前面有一个妇人坐着。

"艾姆，"引她进去的那个小个儿说。"艾姆，是个小姑娘。"她转身对着劳拉。她有意味地说："我是她的妹子，小姐。您得原谅她不是？"

"啊，可是当然。"劳拉说。"请，请不要打搅她。我——我只要放下——"

但是这时候坐在灶火前的妇人转了过来。她的脸子，肿胀着，红红的，红肿的眼，红肿的口唇，看得可怕。她看是摸不清为什么劳拉在那儿。这算什么意思？为什么一个外客拿着一个篮子站在她的厨房里？这是怎么回事？她那可怜的脸子又是紧紧地皱了起来。

"我有数，"还是那个人说。"我会谢小姑娘的。"

她又说了："您得原谅她，小姐，我想你一定。"她的脸子，也是肿肿的，想来一个讨好的笑容。

劳拉只求马上出去，马上走开。她已经回上了那条通道。那门开了。她一直走过去，走进那间卧房，那死人就摊在那里。

"您得看看他不是？"艾姆的妹子说，她匆匆跑上前去到那床边，"不要怕，我的姑娘，"——现在她的口音变得很爱惜，很机敏似的，她爱怜地把死人身上的被单拉下了——"他像一幅画。什么怪相也没有。过来，我的乖。"

劳拉过来了。

一个年轻的人躺在那里，深深地睡着——睡得这样的沉，这样的深，他看是离他们俩远着哪。啊，这样隔着远远的，这样的平静。他在做梦，从此不要惊醒他了。他的头深深地落在枕头上，他的眼紧闭着，眼睛在紧闭了的眼睛子里是盲的了。他全交给他的梦了。什么园会呀，竹篮子呀，花边衣呀，与他有什么相干。他离开那些个事情远着哪。他是神奇的，美丽的了。一面他们在那里欢笑，一面音乐队在那里奏乐，这件不可思议的事到了这条小巷里。快活……快活……什么都好了，睡着的脸子在说。这正是该的。我是满足了。

但是我总得哭一哭，她要出这屋子总得对他说几句话。劳拉响响地孩子似的哭了一声。

"饶恕我的帽子。"她说。

这时候她也不等艾姆的妹子了。她自己走出了门，下了走道，经过那些黑沉沉的人们。在那巷子的转角上她碰着了劳里。

他从黑荫里走了出来。"是你吗，劳拉？"

"是我。"

"娘着急了，没有什么吗？"

"是，很好。啊，劳里！"她挽住他的臂膀，紧紧地靠着他。

"我说，你没有哭不是？"她的兄弟问。

劳拉摇着她的头。她是哭着哩。

劳里拿手围着她的肩膀。"不要哭，"他那亲热的，爱怜的口音说，"那边难受不是？"

"不，"劳拉悲哽地说。"这太不可思议了，但是，劳里——"她停顿了，她望着她的兄弟。"生命是不是，"她打顿地说，"生命是不是——"但是生命是什么她说不上。不碍。他很懂得。

"可不是，乖乖？"劳里说。

毒　药

Poison

邮差来得很迟。我们饭后散步回来了都还没有到。

"还没有哪，太太。"安妮特①唱着，匆匆地跑回去烧菜了。

我们把我们的纸包带进了饭厅。桌子摆好了。每回我看着这两个人的餐具——就只两个人的——来得这整齐，合适，再没有第三者的地位，我就觉得一阵古怪的飞快的寒噤仿佛是叫那银色电光满在白桌布上，亮玻璃杯上，装着兰花的浅瓷盘上，耀动地打着了似的。

"咒那老信差！怎么回事还不来他的？"比阿特丽斯②说。"把东西放下了，亲亲。"

"你要我往哪儿放？"

她抬起她的头；笑她那甜甜的逗人的笑。

"随便哪儿——蠢。"

可是我心上顶明白我决不能随便放，我宁可抱着那肥矮的蜜酒瓶子糖果包儿成月成年地站着，决不能招她爱整齐的细心受一点点的烦腻。

"这儿——交给我吧。"她接了过去连着她的长手套、一小篮的干果往桌上一掷。"饭桌子。短篇小说谁——谁写的？"她拉着我的臂膀。"我们到凉台上去。"——我觉着她震震的。

_____

① ②　为了更加符合现代读者的阅读习惯，本书将原书中民国时期的英文译名"安娜"（Annette）改为现今通行的"安妮特"；"阿梨"（Beatrice）改为"比阿特丽斯"。——编者注

"Ca Sent"，她轻轻地说，"de la Cuisine……"（这儿闻着厨房的味儿。）

我新近留心——我们到南边来有两个月了——她每回要讲到吃食，或是天气，或是闹着玩给我说亲热话，她就说法文。

我们蹲在天棚底下的栏杆上。比阿特丽斯靠着往下望——直沿着那仙人掌镶边的白道儿望。她那耳朵的美，就那耳，美得叫你诧异，我真可以一边看了它转过头去对着底下那一片闪光的海水愣着说："你知道——她的耳！她那一双耳简直是顶……"

她穿一身白的，脖子上套着一串珠子，腰带上插着一把铃兰。她左手的第三个手指上戴一只珠戒——没有结婚戒。

"为什么我用着戴，Mon ami？我们为什么要充？谁在乎来？"

这我当然同意，虽则就私心深处说，我才叫愿意在一个大大的体面的教堂里站在她的一边，背后满挤着人，一个多老多威严的老牧师当差，听那"乐园里的声音"，旁边晃着棕榈叶子，满闻着香味，教堂外面铺着红地毯，还有什么喜糕，香槟，一只缎鞋预备往彩车后背掷的——要是我能把一个结婚戒滑上她的手指。

也不为我稀罕这套讨人厌的铺张，可是我觉得这一来或许可以减少些这"绝对自由"怪味儿的感觉，我意思是她的绝对自由，当然。

喔天！什么刑罚这幸福是——什么痛苦，我望着这庄子看，看我们睡房的窗子顶神秘地在绿色稻草编的窗帘背后躲着。她会不会在那绿光里移动着，笑着她那奥妙的笑，她那懒洋洋亮晶晶专对我的笑？她的手臂钩住了我的脖子；那一只手软软的，骇人的，掠着我的头发。

"你是谁呀？"她是谁呀？她是——"女人"。

……在春天第一个暖和的晚上，灯光像珍珠似的在紫丁香的空气里透亮着，小声音在花鲜鲜的园里嘀咕着，在那里薄纱长帘笼着的高屋里唱着的就是她。那晚在月光下坐车进那外国城子，落在街旁窗扉上闪荡的金光里的是她的影子。上灯的时候，在新来的静定里走进你的门的是她的脚步。回头，摩托车扫着过去的时候，她直瞅着深秋的黄昏，脸白白的，脖子上围着皮……

简单说，那时候我二十四。当她仰面躺着，珍珠项链兜着她的下巴，叹一口气说："我渴了，亲爱的。给我一个橘子。"我真情情愿愿地往水里跳到大鳄鱼牙缝里去拼一个橘子回来——要是鳄鱼口里有橘子的话。

> "我要是有两只毛毛的小翅，
>   是一只毛毛的小雀……"

比阿特丽斯唱着。

我抓住她的手。"你不会飞跑的？"

"不远儿。顶远到那条道儿的尽头。"

"干什么要上那儿去？"

她背诗了："他不来，她说……"

"谁？那笨迟的老邮差？可是你没有望着信。"

"不，可是这叫人着急还不是一样。啊！"忽地她发笑了，紧靠着我。"那儿就是他——看——像一只蓝色的硬壳虫。"

我们俩脸凑得紧紧的，望着那蓝虫子慢慢地爬上来。

"亲爱的，"比阿特丽斯低喘着。那字音像是在空气里耽着不散，震震的像是琴弦上发出来的一个音符。

"怎么了？"

"我不知道，"她软软地笑着。"一阵波浪—— 一阵情爱的波浪，我猜是。"

我伸手圈住了她。"那你不想飞跑了？"

她快快地幽幽地说："不！不！有什么我都不。真的不。我爱这个地方。我爱在这儿耽着。我成年地住下去都能，我信。我从没有过像这两个月快活的时光，你又待我这样好，亲爱的，没一点不如我的意。"

这听来真是极乐——听她说这样话真是难得，从不曾有过的，我得把它笑开了去。

"别！你说话倒像是要分离告别似的。"

"喔，胡说，胡说。再不要你随便说话——说笑也不许！"她的一只小手溜进了我的白外褂，抓住了我的肩膀。"你这一晌乐了不是？"

"乐？乐？喔，天——要是你知道我这会儿的心里……乐！我这奇怪！我这快活！"

我离开了栏杆，抱住了她，把她举在我的怀里。她悬空着，我把我的脸紧偎着她的胸膛低声说："你是我的？"

自从认识她以后，我直着急了这几个月，也算上那一个什么——可不是——登仙的一个月，这回她回答我的话我才第一次完全地相信了：

"是，我是你的。"

门开的声响连着信差上石子路的脚步，分开了我们。一阵子我觉得发眩。我就站在那里微微地笑，自己觉得怪笨相的。比阿特丽斯向着放藤椅子一边走了过去。

"你去——去拿信。"她说。

我——吭——我简直晃了开去。可是我已经太迟了。安妮特跑了来。"没有信。"她说。

我冲着她递报纸给我露出了粗心的笑容准叫她觉着诧异。我快活得什么似的。我把报纸往空中一丢口里唱着：

"没有信，乖乖！"我走近我这心爱的女人躺着的一张长椅子边。

一阵子她没有回话。直到她拉开报纸包皮的时候才慢慢地说："忘了这世界，叫这世界给忘了。"

有好多为难的当儿只要一支烟卷就过得去。它还不止是一个同伴哪；它是一个秘密的，顶合适的小朋友，他这事情全懂得，完全懂得。你抽的时候你望着它——笑或是板脸，看情景起；你深深地吸一口，又慢慢地把那口烟吐了出来。这正是这样一个当儿。我走近那棵木兰①树去，深深地吸那香味。我又走了回来，靠着她的肩膀。可是一阵子她就把手里的报纸往石板上一掷。

"什么都没有，"她说。"没有事。就有一个什么毒药案子。一个男人说是谋杀了他的太太，谁知他是不是，每天有两万人挤在法庭里听审，审过了一次就有两百万字电报满天飞报告新闻。"

"蠢世界！"我说，往一张椅上栽了下去。我心想忘了这报纸，再回到方才信差没上门以前的情形，可是不怎么露痕迹的，当然。但是从她那回话的声音我就知道那时候目前是回不来了。不碍事。我甘愿等着——整五百年都行——反正我现在有拿把了。

"也不怎么蠢，"比阿特丽斯说。"再说这也不能完全是那

---

① 为了更加符合现代读者的阅读习惯，本书将原书中民国时期的英文译名"橡果"（Magnolia）改为现今通行的译名"木兰"。——编者注

两万人方面病理的好奇。"

"是什么呢，乖？"天知道我管他是什么。

"有罪！"她叫着说。"有罪！你明白不明白那个？他们着了迷似的正像是生病人听着了什么关连他们自己病症的消息。囚箱里站着的那个许是够清白的，是在法庭里的群众几乎全是下毒的人。难道你从没有想着过，"——她一兴奋脸色变白了——"这每天有多少毒害的情形？难得有几个结婚的夫妇能保得住不彼此毒害——夫妻们，情人们。喔，"她叫着，"多少杯茶，多少盅酒，多少杯咖啡，全是沾了毒的。单说我自己就有几多，拿在手里喝，心里明白或是不明白——冲着这险。世上还有好多夫妻，"——她发笑了——"没有摧的缘故，就为彼此害怕不敢给那致命的一服。那一服得要你够狠心！可是迟早总免不了。那药一次下了以后你再也不用想往回走。那就是结局的开端，真的，你信不信？你懂不懂我的意思？"

她没等我回话。她拆下了她带上的铃兰花，躺了下去，拿花在她的眼前晃着。

"我的两个男人都毒了我。"比阿特丽斯说。

"我第一个丈夫差不多一结婚就给了我大大的一服，可是我那第二个倒也算是一个美术家。就给一点点儿，隔了一时再给一点点儿，又是顶聪明的，一点也不露痕迹——喔，真聪明！直到一个早上我醒来的时候才明白我浑身直通到手指脚趾尖上，没一个细胞里不含着稀小的一点。我就刚够有时候……"

我就恨她这样坦然地提起她的丈夫，尤其是今天。那叫人难受。我正要说话，她悲声地叫了出来：

"为什么？为什么这事情得轮着我身上？我做了什么来了？为什么我这辈子就叫人说挑出来……那不是串通了害人来了。"

我就对她说那是因为这世界太坏，她太好了——太精，太美，这世界就不容。我插了一个小笑话：

"可是我没有成心来害你。"

比阿特丽斯来了一个古怪的小笑，口咬着一条花梗子。

"你？"她说。"你害不了一个苍蝇！"

怪。那话倒反刺人。顶难过的。

这当儿安妮特给我们拿了饭前开胃酒来。比阿特丽斯靠出身子去从盘上拿了一杯递给我。我留意到我叫珠指的她那手指上的珠子的闪亮。她说那话哪能叫我不难受？

"你，"我说，拿起酒杯，"你从没有毒过谁。"

那话给了我一个意思；我想说明白它。"你——你刚做的反面。叫什么呢？像你这样人，非但不毒人，反而给他们装上——不论谁，信差，替我们赶车的，划船的，卖花的，我——给他们装上新生命，布施她自己的光彩，她的美，她的——"

梦迟迟的她微笑着；梦迟迟的她望着我。

"你想着什么来了——我的可爱的乖乖？"

"我正想着"，她说，"饭后不知道你去不去邮局取下午信。你不介意吗，亲爱的？我并不是等信——可是——我正想着，也许——要是有信不去取可不是傻。对不对？要不然等到明天多傻。"她是看她手指间的玻璃杯梗子。她的美丽的头往下注视着，但我举起了我的杯，喝了，实在是啜着——慢慢地啜着，成心的，眼瞅着那暗蓬蓬的头，心想着——信差，蓝虫子们，告别的话那并不是告别的话，还有——

老天爷！是幻想吗？不，那不是幻想。那酒尝着冷，苦味，怪。

巴克妈妈的行状

Life of Ma Parker

巴克妈妈是替一个独身的文学家收拾屋子的。一天早上那文学家替她开门的时候，他问起巴克妈妈的小外孙儿。巴克妈妈站在那间暗暗的小外房的门席子上，伸出手去帮着他关了门，再答话。"我们昨天把他埋了，先生。"她静静地说。

"啊啊！我听着难过。"那文学家惊讶地说。他正在吃他的早饭。他穿着一件破烂的便袍，一张烂破的报纸，拿在一只手里。但是他觉得不好意思。要不再说一两句话，他不好意思走回他的暖和的"起坐间"去——总得再有一两句话。他想起了他们一班人下葬是看得很重的，他就和善地说："我料想下葬办得好好儿的。"

"怎么说呢，先生？"老巴克妈妈嘎着嗓子说。

可怜的老婆子！她看得怪寒碜的。"我猜想你们下葬办得——办得很妥当吧。"他说。巴克妈妈没有答话。她低着头，蹒跚着走到厨间里去了，手里抓紧着他的老旧的鱼袋，那袋里放着她收拾的家伙，一条厨裙，一双软皮鞋。文学家挺了挺他的眉毛，走回他的房里吃早饭去了。

"太难受了，想是。"他高声地说着，伸手去捞了一块橘酱。

巴克妈妈从她帽子里拔出了两枝长簪，把帽子挂在门背后。她也解开了她破旧的短外衣的衣扣，也挂上了。她捆上了她的厨裙，坐下来脱她的皮靴。脱皮靴或是穿皮靴是她一件苦楚的事，但是她吃这苦楚也有好几年了。其实，她真是吃惯这苦的，每次她连靴带都不曾解散，她的脸子早已拉得长长的，扭得弯弯的，准备那一阵的抽痛。换好了鞋，她叹了口气坐了下去，轻轻地抚摩她的膝部……

"奶奶！奶奶！"她的小孙儿穿着有扣的小皮靴站在她的衣兜上。他方才从街里玩过了进来的。

"看，孩子，你把你奶奶的裙子踹得像个什么样子！你这顽皮的孩子！"

但是他把一双小手臂抱着她的头项，把他的小脸子紧紧地贴着她的。

"奶奶，给我一个铜子！"他讨好地说。

"去你的，孩子；奶奶没有铜子。"

"你有的。"

"不，我没有。"

她已经伸手去摸她的破旧的，压坏的，黑皮的钱包。

"可是孩子你又有什么东西给你的奶奶呢？"他给了一个怕羞的小小的笑靥，小脸子挨得更紧了。她觉得他的眼睫毛在她的腮边跳动着。"我没有什么东西，"他喃喃地说……

老妇人跳了起来，伸手从汽油炉上拿下了铁水壶，走到废物槽边盛水去。开水壶里的沸响好像呆钝了她的心痛似的。她又装满了提桶和洗器盆的水。

没有一本整本的书，也描写不了那厨房的情形。每星期除了星期日那文学家"总算"是自己收拾的。他把用过的茶叶尽朝尽晚地倒在一个果酱瓶里，那是放着专为倒茶叶用的，要是他用完了干净的叉子，就在拉得动的擦手布上篦了一个两个暂时使用。除此以外，他对他的朋友说，他的"系统"是很简单的，他总不懂人家管家就有那么多的麻烦。

"你把你所有的家具全使脏了，每星期叫一个老婆子来替你收拾不就完？"

结果是把厨房弄成了一个巨大的垃圾桶。连地板上满是面包皮屑、信封、烟卷蒂头。但是巴克妈妈倒不怨他。她看这年轻的先生没有人看着他，怪可怜的。从那烟煤熏黑了的窗子望出去只看见一大片惨淡的天，有时天上起了云，那些云也看得像用旧了，老惫了似的，边上擦烂了的，中间有的是破洞，或是用过了茶叶似的暗点子。

一面壶里的水在蒸汽，巴克妈妈拿了帚子扫地。"是的，"她心里想，帚子在地板上碰着，"管他长的短的，我总算有了我的份儿了。我只是劳苦了一辈子。"

就是邻居们也是这么说她。好几回她拿着她的旧鱼袋，蹒跚着走回家的时候，她听他们站在路的转角儿上，或是靠在他们门外的铁栏子上，在说着她："她真是劳苦了一辈子，巴克妈妈真是劳苦了一辈子。"这话真是实在的情形，所以巴克妈妈听了也没有什么得意。好比你说她是住在二十七号屋子的地层的后背，一样的不稀奇。劳苦了一辈子！……

十六岁那年她离了斯特拉特福①，到伦敦做人家厨下帮忙的。是呀，她是生长在埃文河畔的斯特拉特福②的。莎士比亚，先生你问谁呀？不，人家常在问着她莎士比亚这样那样的。但是她却从没有听见过他的名字，直到她后来见了戏馆外面的招贴画。

她的本乡她什么都记不得了，除了"黄昏时候坐在家里火炉边从烟筒里望得见天上的明星"，还有"娘总有一长条的咸肉挂在天花板上的"。还有一点什么——一个草堆儿，有的是——在家门口儿，草香味儿顶好闻的。但是那草堆儿也记不清了。就是有一两次生了病睡在病院里的时候，她记起了那门前的草堆儿。

她第一次做工的人家，是一个很凶的地方，他们从不准她出门。她也从不上楼去，除了早上与晚上的祷告。那地层倒是很整齐的。厨娘待她也很凶。她常抢她没有看过的家信，掷在火灶里毁了，因为怪她看了信总是做梦似的想心事……还有那些蟑螂！你许不信——她没有到伦敦之前，从没有见过一个黑偷油婆儿。

①② 为了更加符合现代读者的阅读习惯，本书将原书中民国时期的英文译名"斯德辣脱福特"（Stratford）改为现今通行的译名"斯特拉特福"，"阿房河上的斯德辣脱福德"改为"埃文河畔的斯特拉特福"。——编者注

每次讲到这儿巴克妈妈总是自己要笑的，好像是……从没有见过一个黑偷油婆儿！得了！这不是比如说你从没有见过你自个儿的脚，一样的可笑。

后来这家人家把房子卖了，她又到一个医生家里去"帮忙"，在那里做了两年早上忙到晚的工以后，她就和她的男人结婚。他是一个面包师。

"他是做面包的，巴克太太！"那文学家就说。因为有时候他也暂时放下他的书本，留心来听她的讲话，讲她的——生平。"嫁一个面包师准是顶有意思的！"

巴克太太的神气没有他那样的有把握。

"这样洁净的生意。"文学家说。

巴克太太还是不大相信。

"你不愿意把新鲜做出来的整块的面包，递给你们的主顾吗？"

"可是，先生，"巴克妈妈说，"我老在地层里，不大上楼到店里去。我们总共有十三个小孩，七个已经埋了。我们的家要不是医院，就是病院，对不对呢？"

"真的是，巴克太太！"文学家说着，耸着肩膀，又把笔拿在手里了。

是的，七个已经去了，剩下的六个还不曾长大，她的丈夫得了肺病，那是面粉入肺，那时医生告诉她……她的丈夫坐在床里，衬衫从后背翻上头，医生的指头在他的背上画了一个圆圈。

"我说，要是我们把他从这里打开，巴克太太，"那医生说，"你就看得见他的肺让白面粉打了一个大洞。呼气试试，我的好朋友！"这儿巴克太太说不清是她亲眼见的或是她的幻想，她见她可怜的丈夫口唇一开就有风车似的一阵白灰冒了出来……

但是她还得奋斗着养大她的六个小孩子，还得奋斗着自个儿过自个儿的活，可怕的奋斗！后来，等到那群孩子稍为长大一点可以上学堂去了，她丈夫的姊妹来伴他们住着帮一点子忙，可是她住不满两个月，她就从楼梯上闪了下来，伤了她的背梁。那五年内巴克妈妈又有了一个孩子——又是一个哭哭啼啼的！——她还得自个儿喂奶。后来玛蒂那孩子没有走正道儿，连着她妹子艾丽丝①都带坏了；两个男孩子上了外洋，小吉姆②到印度当兵去，最小的埃塞尔③嫁了一个一事无成的小堂倌，兰尼④生的那年他生烂疮死了。现在小兰尼我的小外孙儿……

一堆堆的脏杯子，脏盘子，都已洗过，擦干了。墨水似的黑的刀子，先用一片白薯狠劲地擦，再用软木，才擦得干净。桌子已经擦净，食器架与那水槽子一根根沙丁鱼的尾巴在泳着……

----

①②③④ 为了更加符合现代读者的阅读习惯，本书将原书中民国时期的英文译名"阿丽司"（Alice）改为现今通行的译名"艾丽斯"；"杰姆"（Jim）改为"吉姆"；"安稞"（Ethel）改为"埃塞尔"；"来义"（Lennie）改为"兰尼"。——编者注

那孩子从小就不强健——从小就是的。他长得怯怜怜的人家看了都当是女孩子。银白的好看的发鬈儿他有，小蓝眼儿，鼻子的一边有宝石似的一个小斑点儿。养大那孩子，她与她女儿埃塞尔费的劲儿！报上有什么，她们就买了让他读！每星期日的早上埃塞尔高声地念报，一面巴克妈妈洗她的衣服。

"好先生，——我就写一行字让你知道我的小孩梅蒂尔差不多已经死了……用了你的药四瓶……在九星期内长了八磅的重，现在还在继续加重哪。"

念了这类的药广告，架子上盛着墨水的鸡蛋杯就拿了下来，买药的信也写成了，明天早上妈妈去做工的时候乘便就到邮局里去买了一张邮汇单。但是还是没有用。什么法子都不能叫小兰尼加重。就是带了他到惨淡的墓园去，他的小脸子上也比不出一点活泼的颜色，老是那青白的；就是抱了他去坐街车好好地震他一次，回家来他的胃口还是不成。

但是他是奶奶的孩子，原先就是的……

"你是谁的孩子呀？"巴克妈妈说着，伸着腰，从炉灶边走到烟煤熏黑的窗边去了。一个小孩的口音，又亲热，又密切，妈妈几乎气都喘不过来——那小口音好像就在她的胸口，在她的心里——笑了出来，喊说："我是奶奶的孩子！"

正在那个时候来了一阵脚步声，文学家已经穿了衣服预备出门散步去。

"巴克太太，我出去了。"

"是您哪，先生。"

"你的'二先令六'我放在墨水架的小盘上。"

"费心您哪，先生。"

"啊，我倒想起了，巴克太太，"文学家急促地说，"上次你在这儿的时候有些可可你没有掷了吗？"

"没有，先生。"

"很怪，明明有一调羹的可可剩在铁筒子里的，赌咒都成。"他转身走了。他又回头说，和缓地，坚定地，"以后你要掷了什么东西，请你告诉我一声，好不好，巴克太太？"他走了开去，很得意的神气，他自以为他已经让巴克太太明白，别看他样子不精明。他同太太们一样的细心哪。

嘭的一声门关上了。她拿了她的刷子，揩抹布，到卧房里去收拾，但是她在铺床的时候，拉直着，折拢着，轻拍着，她还是忘不了她的小外孙儿，她想着真难受。为什么他要那样的受罪？她总是想不通。为什么一个好好的安琪儿似的小孩，会得连喘气都得同人要，用得着吃那样的大苦。要一个小孩子遭那样的大罪，她看得真没有意思。

……兰尼的小胸膛发出一种声响，像是水在壶里滚沸似的。有一大块的东西老是在他的胸膛里泛泡似的，他怎么也摆脱不了。他一咳嗽，汗就在他的头上钻了出来；他的眼也胀大了，手也震着，他胸口里的一大块就在那里泛泡，像一个白薯在锅子里乱滚似的。这还不算什么，最难受的是他有时也不咳嗽，他就是背着枕头坐着，不说话也不答话，有时竟是连话都听不见似的。他就是坐着，满面的不痛快。

"这可不是你的可怜的老奶奶的不好，我的乖乖。"老巴克妈妈说，在他涨紫了的小耳朵边轻掠着他汗湿了的头发。但是兰尼摇着他的头，避开了去，看得像是和她很过不去似的——脸子还是沉沉的。他低着他的头，斜着眼望着她，像是他不能相信这是他的奶奶似的。

但是到了末了……巴克妈妈把压床被甩着，铺过床去。不，她简直想都不能想。

这是太难了——她一生的命实在是太苦了。她一直忍耐到今天，她，她还得自己顾管自己，也从没有人见她哭过。谁都没有见过，就是她自己的孩子也从没有见过她倒下来。可是现在！兰尼完了——她还有什么？她什么都完了。她过了一辈子就是淘成了一个他，现在他也没有了。为什么这些个儿事情全碰着我？她倒要问。"我做了什么事？"老妈妈说，"我做了什么事？"

她一头说着话，她手里的刷子掉了下去。她已经在厨间里。她心里难受得可怕，她就戴上了她的帽子，穿上了外衣，走出了那屋子，像在梦里似的。她自己也不明白她在干什么。她像是一个人让什么可怕的事吓疯了转身就跑似的——哪儿都好，只要走开了就像是逃出了………

那时街上很冷，风来像冰似的，来往的人快步地走着，很快；男人走着像剪子，女人像猫。没有人知道——也没有人管。即使她倒了下来就便隔了这么多的年份，到底她哭了出来，她着落在哪儿呢——拘留所，也许的。

但是她一想着哭，就像小兰尼跳上了他奶奶的臂膀似的。啊，她就想哭，小团团。奶奶要哭。只要她现在哭得出，一场痛痛快快的大哭，什么都该得哭，一直从她初次做工的地方与那凶恶的厨娘哭起，哭过去哭到第二次做工的那医生家里，再哭那七个早死的小的，再哭她丈夫的死，再哭她走散了的孩子们，再哭以后苦恼的日子，一直哭到小外孙儿兰尼。但是要认真地什么都得哭，一件件的哭，就得有多大的工夫。还是一样，哭的时候已经到了。她总得哭一场。她再不能放着等；她再不能等了……她能上哪儿去呢？

"她是劳苦了一生的，巴克太太。"是的，劳苦了一生，真是！她的腮子颤动起来了；要去就得去了。但是哪儿呢？哪儿呢？

她不能回家；埃塞尔在那儿。她准把埃塞尔的命都啼跑了。她不能随便选一个路凳坐着哭：人家准会过来盘问她。她又不能回到她那先生的屋子去；她不能在旁人的家里放着嗓子号哭。要是她坐在露天的阶沿石级上，就有警察过来对她说话。

啊，难道真是连一个可以自个儿躲起来随她爱耽多久，不麻烦人家，也没有人来"别扭"她的地方都找不到了吗？难道真是在这世界上就没有她可以尽性地哭他一个痛快的地方了吗——到底？

巴克妈妈站定了，向天望望，向地望望：冰冷的风吹着她的厨裙，卷成了一个气球。现在天又下雨了。还是没有地方去。

一杯茶

A Cup of Tea

罗斯玛丽·费尔①并不怎样的美。不，你不会得叫她美。好看？呃是的，要是你把她分开来看……可是为什么要拿一个好好的人分开来看，这不太惨了吗？她年纪是轻的，够漂亮，十分的时新，穿衣服讲究极了的，专念最新出的新书博学极了的，上她家去的是一群趣极了的杂凑，社会上顶重要的人物以及……美术家——怪东西，她自己的"发现"，有几个怕得死人的，可也有看得过好玩的。

罗斯玛丽结婚两年了。她有一个蜜甜的孩子，男的。不，不是彼得——叫迈克尔②。她的丈夫简直是爱透了她的。他们家有钱，真的有钱，不是就只够舒服过去一类，那听着寒碜，闷劲儿的，像是提起谁家的祖老太爷祖老太太。他们可不，罗斯玛丽要什么东西，她就到巴黎去买，不比你我就知道到邦德③街去。她要买花的话，她那车就在雷金特④街上那家上等花铺子门前停住了，罗斯玛丽走进铺子去扁着她那眼，带"洋味儿"的看法，口里说："我要那些那些。那个给我四把。那一瓶子的玫瑰全要。呃，那瓶子也让我带了去吧。不，不要丁香。我恨丁香。那花不是样儿。"铺子里的伙计弯着身子，拿丁香另放在一个看不见的地方，倒像她那话正说对了似的，丁香是真不是样儿。"给我那

---

①②③④ 为了更加符合现代读者的阅读习惯，本书将原书中民国时期的英文译名"费蔷媚"（Rosemary Fell）改为现今通行的译名"罗斯玛丽·费尔"；"密仡儿"（Michael）改为"迈克尔"；"彭德"（Bond）改为"邦德"；"黎锦"（Regent）改为"雷金特"。——编者注

一球矮个儿的郁金香①。那红的白的也拿着。"她走出铺子上车去的时候，就有一个瘦小的女孩子一颠一颠地跟在背后，抱着一个大的白纸包的花，像是一个孩子裹在长抱裙里似的……

一个冬天的下午她在柯曾②街上一家古董铺里买东西。她喜欢那铺子。他那儿先就清静，不提别的，你去往往可以独占，再兼那铺子里的掌柜，也不知怎么的，就爱伺候她。她一进门儿，他不提有多快活。他抱紧了他自个儿的手；他感激得话都说不出来。恭维，当然。可还是的，这铺子有意思……

"你明白，太太，"他总是用他那恭敬的低音调讲话，"我宝贵我的东西。我宁可留着不卖的，与其卖给不识货的主顾，他们没有那细心，最难得的……"

一边深深地呼着气，他手里拿一小方块的蓝丝绒给展开了，放在玻璃柜上，用他那没血色的指尖儿按着。

今天的是一只小盒子。他替她留着的。他谁都没有给看过的。一只精致的小珐琅盒儿，那釉光真不错，看得就像是在奶酪里焙成的。那盖上雕盖一个小人儿站在一株开花的树底下，还有一个更小的小人儿还伸着她那一双手搂着他哪。她的帽子，就够小绣球花的花瓣儿大，挂在一个树枝上；还有绿的飘带。半天里还有一朵粉红的云彩在他们的头顶浮着，像一个探消息的天

<hr>

① ② 为了更加符合现代读者的阅读习惯，本书将原书中民国时期的英文译名"黄水仙"(tulip) 改为现今通行的译名"郁金香"；"寇崇"(Curzon) 改为"柯曾"。——编者注

使。罗斯玛丽把她自己的手从她那长手套里探了出来。她每回看这类东西总是褪了手套的。吮，她很喜欢这个。她爱它；它是个小宝贝。她一定得留了它。她拿那奶光的盒儿翻覆地看，打开了又给关上，她不由地注意到她自个儿的一双手，衬着柜上那块蓝丝绒，不提够多好看。那掌柜的，在他心里那一个不透亮的地基儿，也许竟敢容留同样的感想。因为他手拿着一管铅笔，身子靠在玻璃柜上，他那白得没血色的手指儿心虚虚地向着她那玫瑰色发艳光地爬着，一边他喃喃地说着话："太太你要是许我点给你看，那小人儿的上身衣上还刻着花哪。"

"有意思！"罗斯玛丽喜欢那些花。这要多少钱呢？有一晌掌柜的像是没有听见。这回她听得他低声地说了。"二十八个金几尼，太太。"

"二十八个几尼。"罗斯玛丽没有给回音。她放下了那小盒儿；她扣上了她的手套。二十八个几尼。就有钱也不能……她愣着了。她一眼瞟着了一把肥肥的水壶，像一只肥肥的母鸡蹲在那掌柜的头上似的，她答话的口音还有点儿迷糊的："好吧，替我留着——行不行？我想……"

但是那掌柜的已经鞠过躬，表示遵命，意思仿佛是替她留着是他唯一的使命。他愿意，当然，永远替她留着。

那扇谨慎的门咄地关上了。她站在门外的台阶上，看着这冬天的下午。正下着雨，下雨天就跟着昏，黑夜的影子像灰沙似的在半空里洒下来。空气里有一股冷的涩的味儿，新亮上的街灯看着凄惨。对街屋子里的灯光也是这阴瑟瑟的。它们暗暗地亮着像是惆怅什么。街上人匆匆地来往，全躲在他们可恨的伞子底下。罗斯玛丽觉着一阵子古怪的心沉。她拿手筒窝紧了她的胸口；她心想要有那小盒子一起窝着多好。那车当然在那儿。边街就是的。可是她还耽着不动。做人有时候的情景真叫你惊心，就这从屋子里探身出来看着外边的世界，哪儿都是愁，够多难受。你可不能因此就让打失了兴致，你应当跑回家去，吃他一顿特别预备的茶点。但她正想到这儿的时候，一个年轻的女孩子，瘦的，黑的，鬼影子似的——她哪儿来的？——贴近罗斯玛丽的肘子旁边站着，一个小声音，像是叹气，又像是哭，在说着话："太太，你许我跟你说一句话吧？"

"跟我说话？"罗斯玛丽转过身子去。她见一个小个儿的破烂的女子睁着一双大眼珠，年纪倒是轻的，不比她自己大，一双冻红的手抓着她的领口，浑身发着抖，像是才从凉水里爬起来似的。

"太——太太，"那声音发愣地叫着，"你能不能给我够吃一杯茶的钱？"

"一杯茶？"听那声音倒是直白老实的，一点也不像花子的口气。"那你一个子也没有吗?"罗斯玛丽问。

"没有,太太,"她回答。

"多奇怪!"罗斯玛丽冲着黄昏的微光直瞧,那女子的眼光也向她瞪着。这不比奇怪还奇怪!罗斯玛丽忽然间觉到这倒是个奇遇。竟像是陀思妥耶夫斯基①小说里出来的,这黑夜间的相逢。她就带这女子回家去又怎么呢?她就试演演她常常在小说里戏台上看到的一类事情,看他下文怎么来,好不好呢?这准够令人震惊的。她仿佛听着她自己事后对她的朋友们说:"我简直地就带了她回家。"这时候她走上一步,对她身旁暗沉沉的人影儿说:"跟我回家吃茶去。"

那女子吓得往后退。她给吓得连哆嗦都停了一阵子。罗斯玛丽伸出一只手去,按着她的臂膀。"我不骗你,"她说,微微地笑着。她觉得她的笑够直爽够和气的。"来吧,为什么不?坐了我车一共回家吃茶去。"

"你——你不能是这个意思,太太。"那女子说,她的声音里有苦痛。

"是的哪,"罗斯玛丽叫着。"我是要你。你去我欢喜。来你的。"

---

① 为了更加符合现代读者的阅读习惯,本书将原书中民国时期的英文译名"道施滔奄夫斯基"(Dostoevsky)译为现今通行的译名"陀思妥耶夫斯基"。——编者注

那女子拿她的手指盖住她的口，眼睁得老大地盯着罗斯玛丽。"你——你不是带我到警察局去？"她愣着说。

"警察局！"罗斯玛丽发笑了。"我为什么要那么恶？不，我就要你去暖和暖和，乘便听听——你愿意告诉我的话。"

饿慌了的人是容易带走的。车夫拉开了车门，不一会儿她们在昏沉的街道上飞似的去了。

"得！"罗斯玛丽说。她觉着得胜了似的，她的手溜进了套手的丝绒带。她眼看着她钩住的小俘虏，心里直想说，"这我可带住你了。"她当然是好意。喔，岂但好意。她意思要做给这女子看，叫她相信——这世界上有的是奇怪的事情——神话里仙母是真碰得到的——有钱人是有心肠的，女人和女人是姊妹。她突然转过身子去，说："不要害怕。再说，你有什么可怕的，跟我一同走有什么怕？我们都是女人。就说我的地位比你的好，你就该盼望……"

可是刚巧这时候，她正不知道怎样说完那句话，车子停了，铃子一按，门开了，罗斯玛丽有她那殷勤的姿态，半保护的，简直抱着她似的，把那女子拉进了屋子去。暖和，柔软，光亮，一种甜香味儿，这在她是享惯了的平常不放在心上，这时候看还有那个怎样的领略。有意思极了的。她像是一个富人家的女孩子在她的奶房里，柜子打开一个又一个，纸盒儿放散一个又一个的。

"来，上楼来，"罗斯玛丽说，急于要开始她的慷慨。"上来到我房间里去。"这来也好救出这可怜的小东西，否则叫下人们盯着看就够受的；她们一边走上楼梯，她心里就打算连珍妮①都不去按铃叫她，换衣服什么她自个儿来。顶要紧的事情是要做得自然！

"得！"罗斯玛丽第二次又叫了，她们走到了她那宽大的卧房；窗帘全已拉拢了的，壁炉里的火光在她那套精美的水漆家具，金线的坐垫，淡黄的浅蓝的地毡上直晃耀。

那女子就在靠近门那儿站着；她看昏了的样子。可是罗斯玛丽不介意那个。

"来坐下，"她叫，把她那大椅子拉近了火，"这椅子舒泰。来这儿暖和暖和。你一定冷极了。"

"我不敢，太太。"那女子说，她挨着往后退。

"喔，来吧。"——罗斯玛丽跑过去——"你有什么怕的，不要怕，真的。坐下，等我脱下了我的东西我们一同到间壁屋子吃茶舒服去。为什么你怕？"她就轻轻地把那瘦小的人儿半推似的按进了她的深深的摇床。

---

① 为了更加符合现代读者的阅读习惯，本书将原书中民国时期的英文译名"金儿"(Jeanne) 改为现今通行的译名"珍妮"。——编者注

那女子不做声。她就痴痴地坐着，一双手挂在两边，她的口微微地开着。说实话，她那样儿够蠢的。可是罗斯玛丽她不承认那个。她靠着她的一边，问她："你脱了你的帽子不好？你的美头发全湿了的。不戴帽子舒服得多不是？"

　　这回她听着一声轻极了的仿佛是"好的，太太"，那顶压扁了的帽子就下来了。

　　"我再来帮你脱了外套吧，"罗斯玛丽说。

　　那女子站了起来。可是她一手撑着椅子，就让罗斯玛丽给拉。这可费劲了。她自个儿简直没有动活。她站都站不稳像个小孩，罗斯玛丽的心里不由得想，一个人要旁人帮忙他自己也得稍微，就要稍微，帮衬一点才好，否则事情就为难了。现在她拿这件外套怎么办呢？她给放在地板上，帽子也一起搁着。她正在壁炉架上拿下一支烟卷来，忽然听得那女子快声地说，音是低得可有点儿怪："我对不住，太太，可是我要晕了。我得昏了，太太，要是我不吃一点东西。"

　　"了不得，我怎么的糊涂！"罗斯玛丽奔过去按铃了。

　　"茶！马上拿茶来！立刻要点儿白兰地！"

　　下女来了又去了，可是那女子简直地哭了。"不，我不，不要白兰地。我从来不喝白兰地，我要的就是一杯茶，太太。"她眼泪都来了。

这阵子是又可怕又有趣的。罗斯玛丽跪在她椅子的一边。

"不要哭，可怜的小东西。"她说。

"别哭。"她拿她的花边手帕给她。她真的心里说不出的感动了。她把她的手臂放在那一对瘦削的鸟样的肩膀上。

这来她才心定了点儿，不怕了，什么都忘了，就知道她们俩都是女人，她哽咽着说："我再不能这样儿下去，我受不了这个，我再不能受。我非得自个儿寥寥完事。我再也受不了了。"

"你用不着的。有我顾着你。再不要哭了。你看你碰着我还不是好事情？我们一会儿吃茶，你有什么都对我说，我会替你想法子。我答应你。好了，不哭了。怪累的。好了！"

她果然停了，正够罗斯玛丽站起身，茶点就来了。她移过一个桌子来放在她们中间。她这样那样什么都让给那可怜的小人儿吃，所有的夹肉饼，所有的牛油面包，她那茶杯一空就给她倒上，加奶酪，加糖。人家总说糖是滋补的。她自己没有吃；她抽她的烟，又故意眼往一边看，不叫她对面人觉着羞。

真的是，那一顿小点心的效力够奇怪的。茶桌子一挪开，一个新人儿，一个小个儿怯弱的身材，一头发揉着的，黑黑口唇，深的有光的眼，靠在那大椅子里，一种倦慵慵的神情，对壁炉里的火光望着。罗斯玛丽又点上一支烟；这该是时候谈天了。

"你最后一餐饭是什么时候吃的？"她软软地问。

但正这时候门上的手把转动了。

"罗斯玛丽，我可以进来吗？"是菲利普①。

"当然。"

他进来了。"喔，对不住，"他说，他停住了直望。

"你来吧，不碍，"罗斯玛丽笑着说。"这是我的朋友，密斯——"

"史密斯②，太太，"倦慵慵的那个说，她这会儿倒是异常地镇定，也不怕。

"史密斯，"罗斯玛丽说。"我们正要谈点儿天哪。"

"喔，是的。""很好，"说着他的眼瞟着了地板上的外套和帽子。他走过来，背着火站着。"这下半天天时太坏了，"他留神地说，眼睛依然冲着倦慵慵的那个看，看她的手，她的鞋，然后再望着罗斯玛丽。

"可不是，"罗斯玛丽欣欣地说，"下流的天气。"

菲利普笑了他那媚人的笑。"我方才进来是要，"他说，"你跟我到书房里去一去。你可以吗？密斯史密斯许我们不？"

那一对大眼睛蜓了起来瞅着他，可是罗斯玛丽替她答了话。"当然她许的。"他们俩一起出房去了。

_____

①② 为了更加符合现代读者的阅读习惯，本书将原书中民国时期的英文译名"菲立伯"（Philip）改为现今通行的译名"菲利普"；"司密司"（Smith）改为"史密斯"。——编者注

"我说，"菲利普到了书房里说，"讲给我听。她是谁？这算什么意思？"

罗斯玛丽，嘻嘻地笑着，身体靠在门上说："她是我在柯曾街上捡了来的，真的是。她是一个真正的'捡来货'。她问我要一杯的茶钱，我就带了她回家。"

"可是你想拿她怎么办呢？"

"待她好，"罗斯玛丽快快地说。"待她稀奇地好。顾着她。我也不知道怎么了。我们还没有谈哪。可是指点她——看待她——使她觉着——"

"我的乖乖孩子，"菲利普说，"你够发疯了，你知道。哪儿有这样办的。"

"我知道你一定这么说，"罗斯玛丽回驳他。"为什么不？我要这么着。那还不够理由？再说，在书上不是常念到这类事情。我决意——"

"可是，"菲利普慢吞吞地说，割去一支雪茄的头，"她长得这十二分好看。"

"好看？"罗斯玛丽没有防备他这一来，她脸都红了。"你说她好看？我——我没有想着。"

"真是的！"菲利普划了一根火柴。"是简直可爱。再看看去，我的孩子。方才我进你屋的时候我简直地看迷糊了。但是……我想你事情做错了。对不起，乖乖，如其我太粗鲁了或是什么。可是你得按时候让我知道密斯史密斯跟不跟我们一起吃晚饭，我吃前还要看看衣饰杂志哪。"

"你这怪东西！"罗斯玛丽说，她走进了书房，又不回她自己房里去，他走进她的书写间去，在他的书台边坐下了。好看！简直可爱！看迷糊了！她的心像一个大皮球似的跳着，好看！可爱！她手拉着她那本支票簿。可是不对，支票用不着的，当然。她打开一个抽屉，拿出了五张镑票看了看，放回了两，把那三挤在手掌心里，她走回她卧房去了。

半小时以后菲利普还在书房里，罗斯玛丽进来了。

"我就来告诉你，"她说，她又靠在门上，望着他，又是她那扁眯着，眼带"洋味儿"的看法，"密斯史密斯今晚不跟我们吃饭了。"

菲利普放下了手里的报。"喔，为什么了？她另有约会？"

罗斯玛丽过来坐在他的腿上。"她一定要走，"她说，"所以我送了那可怜人儿一点儿钱。她要去我也不能勉强她不是？"她软软地又加上一句。

罗斯玛丽方才收拾了她的头发，微微地添深了一点她的眼圈，也戴上了她的珠子。她伸起一双手来，摸着菲利普的脸。

"你喜欢我不？"她说，她那声音，甜甜的，也有点儿发粗。

"我喜欢你极了，"他说，紧紧地抱住她。"亲我。"

隔了一阵子。

罗斯玛丽迷离地说。"我见一只有趣的小盒儿。要二十八个几尼哪。你许我买不？"

菲利普在膝盖上颠着她。"许你，你这会花钱的小东西。"他说。

可是那并不是罗斯玛丽要说的话。

"菲利普，"那低声地说，她拿他的头紧抵着她的胸膛，"我好看不？"

幸　福

Bliss

贝莎·扬①年纪虽则有三十岁，可是她有时还老想跳着走路，在走道上一上一下地跳舞，赶铁圈子，把手里东西往半空掷上去落下来再用手接，或是站定了不动憨笑着看——没有什么——干脆什么也没有。

你有什么想法，如其你到了三十岁年纪，每回转过你家的那条街的时候，忽然间一阵子的快活——绝对的快活！——淹住了你——仿佛你忽然间吞下了一大块亮亮的那天下午的太阳光，在你的胸口里直烧，发出一阵骤雨似的小火星，塞住你浑身的毛窍，塞住你一个个手指，一个个脚趾……

啊，难道除了这"醉醺醺乱糟糟的"再没有法子表现那点子味儿？多笨这文明，为什么给你这身体，如其你非得把它当一张贵重，贵重的琴似的包起来收好？

"不，我的意思不是拿琴来比，"她想，跑上了家门前的阶石伸手到提包里去摸门上的钥匙——她忘了带，照例地——打着门上的信箱叫门。"我意思不是这样，因为——多谢你，玛丽②"——她进了客厅。"奶妈回来了没有？"

"回来了，太太。"

"水果送来了没有？"

---

①② 为了更加符合现代读者的阅读习惯，本书将原书中民国时期的英文译名"杨培达"（Bertha Young）改为现今通行的译名"贝莎·扬"；"曼丽"（Mary）改为"玛丽"。——编者注

"送来了，太太。东西全来了。"

"请你把水果拿饭间里来。我来收拾了再上楼。"饭间里已经发黑，也觉着凉。但是贝莎还是一样把外套脱了；她厌烦这裹得紧紧的，一股凉气落在她的胳膊上。

但是在她的胸口那亮亮发光的一块还在着——那一阵骤雨似的小火星。简直有点儿受不住。她气都不敢喘，怕一扇动那火更得旺，可是她还是喘着气，深深的，深深的。她简直不敢对着那冰凉的镜子里照——可是她还是照了，镜子里回给她一个女人，神采飞扬的，有带笑容的微震着的口唇，有大大的黑黑的眼珠，她那神气像是听着什么，等着什么——大喜事快到似的——那她知道一定会来——靠得住的。

玛丽把水果装上一个盘子拿了进来，另外带着一只玻璃缸，一只蓝瓷盆子，可爱极了的，上面有一层异样的光彩像是在奶酪里洗过澡似的。

"我把灯开上好不好，太太？"

"不，多谢你。我看得很清楚。"

水果是小宽皮橘、大苹果夹着红色的樱桃。几只黄色的梨，绸子似的光滑，几穗白葡萄发银光的，还有一大串紫葡萄。这紫的她买了来专为给饭间里地毯配色的。是呀，这话听着快有点可笑，可是她买来的意思是那样。她在铺子里就想了："我得要点儿紫的去把地毯挪上桌子来。"她当时也还顶得意的。

她一收拾好，把这些圆圆的亮亮的个儿堆成两个宝塔，她就离着桌子站远一点看看神气——那神气真有味儿。因为这来那暗色的桌子就像化成暗色的天光，那玻璃盘跟蓝碟子就像是在半空里流着。这，冲她这时候的高兴看来，当然是说不出的美……她发笑了。

"不，不成。我又不是疯了。"她就抓了她的提包、她的外套，一直跑上楼到奶妈房里去。

小囡囡洗过了澡，奶妈坐在一张矮桌子一边喂她吃晚饭。囡囡身上穿着白法兰绒①的长衣蓝毛绒的外褂，她的好看的黑头发梳成了一个可笑的小山峰。她见妈进来就仰着头看，耸着身子跳。

"看着，我的乖囡，乖孩子吃完了这点儿。"奶妈说，她那嘴唇皮的样儿贝莎明白，意思说你来看孩子又不是时候。

"她好不好，奶妈？"

"她这下半天是好极了的，"奶妈低声说。"我们同到公园里去，我坐在一张椅子上，把她从推车里拿出来，一只大狗走过来把它的头放在我的腿上，她一把抓住了它的耳朵，使劲地拉。喔，你没见着她那样子。"

贝莎想要问让孩子拉着一只不熟的狗耳朵有没有危险。但是

<hr>

① 为了更加符合现代读者的阅读习惯，本书将原书中民国时期的英文译名"弗赖绒"(flannel) 改为现今通行的译名"法兰绒"。——编者注

她没有敢。她站着看她们，她的手两边挂着，像是一个怪可怜的穷孩子站在一个手抱着洋娃娃的阔孩子跟前发愣似的。

囡囡又抬起头来看她，瞅着她，笑得那美劲儿贝莎不由得叫了出来：

"喔，奶妈，你就让我喂着她，你也好去收拾洗澡东西。"

"吭，太太，她吃的时候，实在是不换手的好，"奶妈说，还是低声的。"一换手，她就乱；她心慌都会的。"

这多可笑。要孩子干吗了？要是她老是得让——不是像一张贵重，贵重的琴似的收在盒子里——另外一个女人抱着？

"喔，我一定得喂。"她说。

气极了的，奶妈把孩子递了给她。

"好了，喂完了饭你可再不能逗她。你知道你老逗她，太太。你一逗她晚上苦着我！"

喔皇天！奶妈拿了洗澡布出屋子去了。

"啊，这会儿我带住了你了，我的小宝贝。"贝莎说，囡囡靠在她的身上。

她吃得顶高兴，掬着她的小嘴等调羹，再来，就甩着小手。有时她含住了不让调羹回去；有时候，贝莎刚给兜满了送过去，她那小手这一推就给泼了。

汤吃过了，贝莎转过去对着壁炉。

"孩子乖——真好孩子！"她说，亲着她的热火火的囡囡。"我喜欢你，我疼你。"

小贝贝她真的爱——她脑袋往前冲露着小颈根，她那精致极了的小脚趾在火光里透明似的发亮——这来她那一阵快活又回来了，她又不知道怎么才好——不知道拿它怎么办。

"太太您有电话。"奶妈说，得胜似的回进房来把她的小贝贝抢了去。

她飞奔了下去。哈利①的电话。

"喔，是你，贝？听着。我得迟点儿来。回头我要个车来尽快赶到，可是你开饭得迟十分钟——成不成？算数？"

"好，就这样。喔，哈利！"

"怎么了？"

她有什么说的？她什么也没得说的。她就想跟他纠缠一会儿。她总不能凭空叫着："这天过得多美呀！"

"怎么回事了？"话筒子里小声音在跳响。"没有事。好了！"贝莎说，挂上了听筒，心想这文明比蠢还蠢。

他们约了人来吃饭。诺曼·奈特夫妇②——一对好夫妻——他正在经营一个剧场，她专研究布置家庭；一个年轻人，埃迪·沃伦③，他新近印了一小册的诗，谁都邀他吃饭；还有一个叫珀尔·富尔顿④的是贝莎的一个"捡着的"朋友。密斯富尔顿

---

①②③④ 为了更加符合现代读者的阅读习惯，本书将原书中民国时期的英文译名"哈雷"（Harry）改为现今通行的译名"哈利"；"那家的"（Norman Knight）改为"诺曼·奈特"；"安迪华伦"（Eddie Warren）改为"埃迪·沃伦"；"珠儿傅敦"（Pearl Fulton）改为"珀尔·富尔顿"。——编者注

做什么事的，贝莎不知道。她们在俱乐部里会着，贝莎一见就爱上了她，那是她的老脾气，每回碰着漂亮女人带点儿神秘性的她就着。

顶招人的一点是虽则她们常常在一起，也曾真真地谈过天，贝莎还是懂不得她。到某一点为止密斯富尔顿是异常的，可爱的直爽，但是那某一点总是在那儿，她到那儿就不过去了。

再过去有什么没有呢？哈利说"没有"。评她无味，"那冷冰冰的劲儿，凡是好看的女人总是那样，也许她有点儿贫血，神经不灵的"。但是贝莎不很同意他，至少现在还不能同意。

"不，她坐着那样儿，头侧在一边，微微地笑，就看出她背后有事情，哈利，我一定得知道她究竟有什么回事。"

"也许是她的胃强。"哈利回答说。

他就存心说这样话来浇贝莎的冷水……"肝发冻了，我的乖孩子"，或是"胃气胀"，或是"腰子病"一类语。说也怪贝莎就爱这冷劲儿，她就佩服他这一下。

她跑客厅里去生上了火；再把玛丽放得好好的椅垫榻垫一个一个全给捡在手里，再往回掷了上去。这来味儿就不同；这间屋子就活了似的。她正要掷回顶末了的一个，她忽然情不自禁地抱住了它往胸前紧紧地挤一挤。但这也没有扑灭她心头的火。呒，更旺了！

客厅外面是走廊，窗子开出去正见花园。那边靠墙的一头，有一株高高的瘦瘦的白梨树，正满满地艳艳地开着花；它那意态看得又爽气又镇静的，冲着头顶碧匀匀的天。这在贝莎看来简直满是开得饱饱的花，一个骨朵儿一朵烂的都没有。地下花坛里的郁金香，红的紫的，也满开着，像是靠着黄昏似的。一只灰色的猫，肚子贴着地，爬过草地去，又一只黑的，它的影子，在后面跟。贝莎看了打了一个寒噤。

"猫这东西偷爬爬的多难看！"她结巴地说着，从窗口转过身来，在屋子里来回地走着。

那长寿花①在暖屋子里味儿多强。太强？喔，不。但她还像是叫花味儿熏了似的，把身子往榻上一倒，一双手紧扪着眼。

"我是太快活了——太快活了！"她低声说。

她仿佛在她的眼帘上看出那棵满开着花美丽的白梨树象征她自己的生活。

真的——真的——她什么都有了。她年纪是轻的。哈利跟她还是同原先一样的热，俩人什么都合适，真是一对好伙计。她有了一个怪可疼的孩子。他们也不愁没有钱。这屋子、这园又多对劲，再好也没有了。还有朋友——新派的、漂亮的朋友，著作家、诗人、画家，或是热心社会问题的——正是他们要的一类朋

① 为了更加符合现代读者的阅读习惯，本书将原书中民国时期的英文译名"寿菊"（jonquil）改为现今通行的译名"长寿花"。——编者注

友。此外还有书看，有音乐听，还找着了一个真不错的小裁缝①，还有到了夏天他们就到外国旅行去，还有他们的新厨子做的煎蛋卷②真好吃……

"我是痴子。痴了！"她坐了起来；可是她觉着头眩，醉了似的。一定是春困的缘故。

是呀，这是春天了。她这会儿倦得连上楼去换衣服都没了劲儿了。

一身白的，一串碧玉珠子，绿的鞋，绿的袜子。这也不是有心配的。她早几个钟头就想着这配色了。

她的衣瓣悚悚地响进了客厅，上去亲了亲诺曼·奈特太太，她正在脱下她那怪好玩的橘色的外套，沿边和前身全是黑色的猴子。

"……唉！唉！为什么这中等阶级总是这么古板——一点点子幽默都没有！真是的，总算是运气好我到了这儿了——亏得诺曼③有他保驾。因为满车子人全叫我的乖猴子们给弄糊涂了，有一个男人眼珠子都冒了出来，像要吞了我似的。也不笑——也不觉着好玩——我倒不介意他们笑，他们偏不。不，就这样呆望着，望得我厌烦死了。"

①②③ 为了更加符合现代读者的阅读习惯，本书将原书中民国时期的英文译名"成衣"（dressmaker）改为"裁缝"；"炒鸡子"（omelette）改为"煎蛋卷"；"脑门"（Norman）改为现今通行的译名"诺曼"。——编者注

"可是顶好笑的地方是，"诺曼说，拿一个大个儿的玳瑁壳镶边的单眼镜安进了他的眼，"我讲这你不嫌不是，费斯？"（在他们家或是当着朋友他们彼此叫费斯与麦格）顶好笑的地方是后来她烦急了转过身去对她旁边的一个女人说："你以前就没有见过猴子吗？'"

　　"喔可不是！"诺曼太太加入笑了，"那真是笑死人不是？"

　　还有更可笑的是现在她脱了外套她那样子真像是一个顶聪明的猴子——里面那身黄绸子衣服像是拿刮光了的香蕉皮给做的。还有她那对琥珀的耳环子，活宕宕的像是两个小杏仁儿。

　　门铃响了。来的是瘦身材苍白脸的埃迪·沃伦，神情异常的凄惨（他总是那样子的）。

　　"这屋子是的，是不是？"他问。

　　"喔，可不是——还不是。"贝莎高兴地说。

　　"我方才对付那汽车夫真窘急了我；再没有那样恶形的车夫。我简直没有法儿叫他停。我愈急愈打着叫他，他愈不理愈往前冲。再兼之在这月光下，他那怪样子扁脑袋蹲在那小轮盘上……"

　　他打了一个寒噤，拿下了一个厚大的白丝围巾。贝莎见着他袜子也是白的——美极了。

"那真是要命。"她叫着。

"是呀，真是的，"艾迪说，跟她进了客室。"我想象我坐着一辆无时间性的汽车，在无空间性的道上赶着。"

他认识诺曼夫妇。他正打算想写一本戏给他们未来的新剧场用。

"唉，沃伦，那戏怎么了？"诺曼·奈特说，吊下了他的单眼镜，给他那一只眼一会儿张大的机会，上了片子就放小了。

诺曼太太说："喔，沃伦先生，这袜子够多写意？""你喜欢我真高兴，"他说，直瞅着他的脚。"这袜子自从月亮升起以后看白得多。"他转过他的瘦削的忧愁的年轻的脸去对着贝莎。"是有月亮，你知道。"

她想叫着："可不是有——常有——常有！"

他真的是顶叫人喜欢的一个人。可是费斯也何尝不然，钻在她香蕉皮里蹲在炉火面前，麦格也有趣，他抽着烟卷，敲着烟灰说话："新官人为什么这慢吞吞的？"

"啊，这是他来了。"

嘭地前门开了又关上。哈利喊着："喂，你们全来了。五分钟就下来。"他们听他涌上了楼梯去。贝莎不由得笑了，她知道他做事就爱逼得紧紧的。说来这另加的五分钟有什么关系？他可得自以为是十二分的重要。他还得拿定主意走进客厅来的时候神气偏来得冷静、镇定。

哈利做人就这有兴味。她最喜欢他这一点。还有他奋斗的精神——他就爱找反抗他的事情作为试验他的胆力的机会——那一点，她也领会。就是在有时候在不熟识他的人看来似乎有点可笑……因为有时他搀起了手臂像打架实际上可并没有架打……她一头笑一头讲直到他进屋子来她简直地忘了珀尔·富尔顿还没有到。

"怕是富尔顿小姐忘了吧！"

"许会的，"哈利说。"她有电话没有？"

"啊！来了一个车。"贝莎微微地笑着，她那带着点子"屋主人"得意的神气的笑当着她的"找着的"女朋友还没有使旧还带神秘性的时候。"她是在汽车里过日子的。"

"那她就会发胖"，哈利冷冷地说，拉铃叫开饭。"漂亮女人顶可怕的危险。"

"哈利——不许。"贝莎警告着，对他笑着。

他们又等着一小会儿，说着笑着，就这一点点子过于舒服，过于随便的样子。富小姐进来了，一身银色衣服，头上用银丝线笼住她的浅色的美头发，笑吟吟的，头微微地侧在一边。

"我迟了罢？"

"不，刚好，"贝莎说。"大家来。"她挽了她的手臂，他们一起走进饭间里去。

碰着她那冷胳膊的时候贝莎觉着点也不知什么它能扇旺——扇旺——放光——放光——那快活的火她不知道怎么办才好？

富尔顿小姐没有对她看；可是她很难得正眼对人看的。她的厚厚的眼睑裹住她的眼，她的异样的半笑不笑的笑在她的口唇上来了又去，正如她平常就用耳听不用眼看似的。但是贝莎知道，不期然的，就同她们俩曾经相互长久地款款的对视——就同她们俩已经对彼此说过："啊你也是的？"——她知道珀尔·富尔顿在搅动淡灰色盘子里美美的红色汤的时候也正觉着她所觉着的。

还有别人呢？费斯与麦格，艾迪与哈利，他们的调羹一起一落的——拿手布擦着嘴，手捏着面包，捻着叉子擎着杯，一路说着话。

"我在阿尔法①赛会上见着她的——怪极了的一个人。她不但铰了她的头发，看神气倒像她连她的腿、她的胳膊、她的脖子、她的怪可怜儿的小鼻子都给剪子抹平了似的。"

"她不是跟迈克尔·奥特②顶密切的不是？"

"就是写《假牙中的恋爱》那个人？"

"他要写个戏给我。一幕。一个男人。决意自杀。列数他该死与不该死的缘由。正当他快要决定他还是干还是不干——幕下。意思也顶不坏。"

"他想给那戏题什么名字叫'肚子痛'？"

"我想我在一个法国小戏里看到过同样的意思——在英国不很有人知道。"

不，在他们间没有那一点子。他们都是有趣的——趣人——她乐意邀他们来，一起吃饭，给他们好饭好酒吃喝。她真的想撑开了对他们说她怎样爱他们的风趣，这群人聚在一起多有意味，色彩各个不同的，怎样使她想起契诃夫的一个戏！

哈利正受用着他的饭。这就是他的——是的，不定是他的本性，不完全是，可决不是他的装相——他的——就是这么回事——爱这讲吃食，顶得意他那"爱吃龙虾的白肉的不知耻的馋欲"，还有"阿月浑子冰冻上面那一层绿——又绿又冷的像是埃及①跳舞女人们的眼皮"。

当他仰起头向着她说："贝莎，这奶冻真不坏！"她快活得孩子似的连眼泪都出来了。

喔，为什么她今晚对着这世界来得这样的心软？什么东西都是好的——都是对的。碰着的事情都仿佛是可把她那快活的杯子

---

① 根据原文的英文"Egyptian"，此处的"土耳其"应改译为"埃及"。——编者注

给盛满了。

可还是的，在她的脑后头，总是那棵梨花树。这会儿该是银色了，在可怜的艾迪的月光下，银得像富尔顿小姐似的银，她坐在那儿翘着她那瘦长的手指儿玩着一只小橘子，多光多白的手指看得漏光似的。

她简直想不透的一点——那简直是神妙——是怎么的她就会猜中珀尔·富尔顿的心，猜得这准这飞快。因为她从不疑问她猜得对，可是她有什么凭据呢，比没有还没有。

"我想这在女人间是很——很少有的。男人更不用提了，"贝莎心里想。"可是回头我到客厅去倒咖啡的时候也许她会'给我一点消息'。"

这话怎么讲她也不知道，以后便怎么样她也不能想象。

她一面想着，一面见她自己笑着说着话。她因为要笑所以得讲话。

"我不打哈哈，怎么着。"

但是当她注意到费斯老是拿什么东西往她的紧身里塞似的那怪脾气——倒像是她那儿也有一个藏干果的小皮袋——贝莎急得把手指甲在她的手背上直掏，单怕撑不住笑太过分了。

好容易饭席散了。"来看我的新咖啡炉子。"贝莎说。

"我们也就每两星期换一架新的。"哈利说。这回费斯挽了她的臂膀；富小姐低下了头，在后面跟着。

客厅里的火已经熄成了一个红的跳光的"小凤凰的窠"，费斯说。

"等会儿再开灯。就这光可爱。"她又在炉火前蹲了下去。"她总是冷的……当然是为没有穿她那件小红法兰绒衫子。"贝莎想。

正那时候富小姐"给消息"了。

"你们有园吗？"那冷冷的带睡意的声音说。

这来太美了，贝莎只能顺着她的意思。她走过一边去，拉开了窗幔，打开了长窗。

"这不是。"她喘着气。

这来她们俩站在一起看着那棵瘦小的满花的树。园里虽是静定，那树看得，像一枝蜡的焰头，在透亮的空气里直往上挺，走着上去，跳动着，愈长愈高了似的冲她们瞅着——差点儿碰着那圆的银色的月的圆边儿了。

她们俩在那儿站了有多久，就比是在那天光的圈子里耽着，彼此间完全相知，同是另一个世界的人，正不知怎么才好，两人心口里全叫这幸福的宝贝给烧得亮亮的，朵朵的银花从她们的发上手上直往下掉？

永远这——在一刹那间？富尔顿小姐她不是低声在说："是

的。就是那个？"还是贝莎的梦想？

灯光捻上了，费斯调着咖啡，哈利说："我的好奈特太太，我们孩子的事情不用问我。我从来不见她的。要我对她发生兴趣，总得等她有了爱人以后吧。"麦格把他的单眼解放了一会儿又把那玻璃片给盖上了，埃迪·沃伦喝了他的咖啡放下杯子去，脸上满罩着忧伤像是喝醉了酒看见了蜘蛛似的。

"我的意思是要给年轻人们一个机会。我相信伦敦市上多的是真头等没写起的剧本。我要对他们说的话是：'戏场现成在这儿。干你们的。'"

"亲爱的，你知道我要去替雅各布·内森①家给布置一间屋子。喔，我多么想来一个'煎鱼'主意试试，拿椅子的后背全给做成煎盘形，幔子上都给来上一条条的灼白薯的绣花。"

"现在我们的年轻的写东西人的一个毛病是他们还嫌太浪漫。你要到大洋里去你就得抵拼晕船要吐盆。那也成，为什么他们就没有吐盆的勇气？"

"那首骇人的诗讲一个女孩子叫一个没有鼻子的讨饭在一个小——小林子里毁了……"

富尔顿小姐在一张最矮最深的椅子上沉了下去，哈利递烟

---

① 为了更加符合现代读者的阅读习惯，本书将原书中民国时期的英文译名"耐登"（Jacob Nathan）改译为"雅各布·内森"。——编者注

卷儿转过来。

看他那站在她面前手摇着银盒子快声地说"埃及？土耳其？弗吉尼亚①？全混着"的神气，贝莎就明白她不仅招他烦，他简直不喜欢她；她又从富小姐的回话："不，多谢，我不吸烟"，认定她也觉着了并且心里难受。

"喔，哈利，不要厌烦她。你对她满不公平。她是太——太有意思了。再说她是我喜欢的人，你先就不能这冷劲儿地对她。回头我们上了床等我来告诉你今晚的情形。她跟我彼此灵通的那一点子。"

就冲这末了的几句话突然间有一点子古怪的，吓得人的什么直透过贝莎的脑筋。这点子瞎眼的带笑容的什么低低地对她说："一会儿客就散了。一会儿屋子就静——静静的。灯全关上了。就剩你与他两口子一起在黑屋子里——那暖烘烘的床……"

她从座椅里跳了起来跑到琴那边去了。

"没有人弹琴多可惜呀！"她叫着。又"多可惜没有人弹"。

在她一辈子她第一次觉着她"要"她丈夫。

喔，她是爱他——当然咾，她别的哪一件事不爱着他，可是就差"这一件"。她也明白，当然，比方说吧，他同她是两样的。他们研究这问题也不止一回了。她最初发现她自己这样的冷，她也很发愁，但过了一时也就惯了，没有什么交关似的。他们彼此间什么话都撑开了说——多好的一对。那就是新派人的好处。

可是这会儿——这火热的！火热的！单这字就叫她火热的身体发痛。难道这就是方才心里说不出的快活的结果？可是那就那就——

"亲爱的，"诺曼·奈特太太说，"你知道我们的可怜。我们少不了做时间跟车的奴隶。我们住在汉普斯特德。今晚真可乐。"

"我陪着你到外厅去，"贝莎说。"我爱你们。可是你们不能误了末一次的车。那真是腻烦不是？"

"来一杯威士忌，奈特，先不要走。"哈利在叫。

"不，谢谢了，老朋友。"

贝莎真感谢他没有耽下来，在她的握手里表示了。

"好睡，再会了。"她从最高那石级上叫着，心里觉着这一个她跟他们从此再会了。

她回进客厅的时候别人也已经在动了。

"……那么你可以乘我的车走。"

"那太好了，省得我单身坐车再来冒险，方才来时候已经上了当。"

"路头就有车。走不到几步路。"

"那合适。我穿外套去。"

富尔顿小姐向外厅走着，贝莎正想跟，哈利几乎挤着走上了她前。

"我来帮你忙。"

贝莎知道他懊悔方才的傲慢了——她由他去，他多像个孩子，有地方——就这任性的——就这——简单的。

火跟前就剩了艾迪跟她。

"我不知道你有没有见过毕尔克士的新诗叫做《公司菜》，"艾迪软软地说。"那诗太好了。在最新出的一本诗选里。你有那本子没有？我一定得指给你看。第一行就是不可思议的美：'为什么那总得是番茄汤'？""有的"，贝莎说。她站起来不出声息地走到正对客厅门那一张桌子边去，艾迪也不出声息地跟着她，她捡着了那本小册子，递给了他：他们一点没有出声。

他仰起头来的当儿她转过她的头去正对着外厅。她看见……哈利拿着富小姐的外套，富小姐背着他，低着头。他把手里的外套一扔，把手放在她的肩膀上，强烈地转过她来向着他。他的口里说："我爱你！"富小姐拿她月光似的手指放在他的脸上，笑了笑她那带睡态的笑。哈利的鼻孔跳动着；他扭着他的嘴唇，怪丑相的口里低低地说："明天。"接着富小姐扬着她的眼皮说："好。"

"在这儿了，"艾迪说。"为什么那总得是番茄汤，这意思真是对，深刻极了，你觉不觉得？番茄汤！永远是那番茄汤。"

"你要的话，"哈利的声音很响亮地在外厅说："我可以打电话叫车到门口来。"

"喔不。用不着。"富尔顿小姐说，她走上来拿她的瘦长手指给贝莎握一握。

"再会，真多谢你。"

"再会。"贝莎说。

富小姐握着她的手较久一点。

"你那棵可爱的梨花树！"她吞吐地说。

她走了，后面跟着艾迪，像那黑猫跟着灰猫。

"我来上店板。"哈利说，过分的冷，过分的镇定。

"你那棵可爱的梨花树——梨花树——梨花树！"

贝莎简直地跑到那长窗子一边去。

"喔，这来下文是什么呢？"她叫着。

但那梨花树还是照样可爱，原先一样的满开着花，一样的静定。

一个理想的家庭

An Ideal Family

那天下午老尼夫①先生捱出了（他公司的）回转门，步下三道的石级，踏上边道，迎着满街的春意，才知道，生平第一遭，他的确是老了——老不禁春了。春，又暖和，又殷勤，又匆忙的春，已经来了，吹弄他的白须，温存地搂着他的臂腕，他却是对付不了，他如今老了，再不能拉整衣襟，向前迈步，青年的飒爽，他没有了，他是乏了，那时晚照虽浓，他却觉得寒噤遍体。

霎时间他没有了精力，他再没有精神来对付明畅活泼的春，春情转把他缠糊涂了。他想止步不前，想把手杖来挥散春光，想喝一声"走你们的"！霎时间他没有了精力，就是一路照例的招呼，把手杖来轻点着帽檐，招呼一路的朋友、相识、店伙、邮差、车役，他亦觉得老大不自在。他往常心里爽快时，喜笑的斜瞬总连着殷勤的手势，仿佛说"别看我老，我比你们谁都强些"——如今他连这一比一瞬都办不了了。他跄跄地走着，把膝部提得高高的，仿佛他在走过的空气，像水般变重了变成实质了似的，那时正值散市，一路匆匆的满是归家的人，街车不住的叮当，小车不住的咔嗒，汽车摇着巨大的躯体，滚旋地前进，那样漫不经心的冲窜，只是梦想的。

那天在公司里，一切如常，没有发生什么事，哈罗德②饭后到将近四点才回。他去哪里了呢？他干什么了？他不会让他爹知道。老尼夫先生碰巧在前廊送客，哈罗德荡着大步进来了，老是他那神气，从容，娴雅，唇边挂着他那最讨女人喜欢似笑非笑的笑。

啊！哈罗德太漂亮了，实在是太漂亮了，种种的麻烦就为的是那个。男子就不应该有那样的眼，那样的睫，那样的口唇；真的怪。他的娘，他的姊妹，家里的仆役，简直把他捧之为神明；他们崇拜哈罗德，什么事都饶恕他；他从十三岁起就不老实，那年偷了他娘的钱包，拿了钱，把空钱包藏在厨子的房里。

老尼夫先生走着，想起了他，不觉狠狠地用手杖捶着走道的边儿。他又回想哈罗德也不单让家里人给宠坏了，不，他的坏什么人都有份，他只要对人一看一笑，人家就会跑到他的跟前，所以无怪他竟整个的公司也着他的魔。哼，哼！那可不成，做生意不是闹着玩，就是根柢打稳准发财的大公司，也不能让闹着玩，要做生意，就得一心一意去做，要不然什么好生意都会眼看着失败。可是一面夏洛特①同女孩子们整天的觉着他，要他把生意整个交给哈罗德，要他息着，享自己的福，自个儿享福！老尼夫先生越想越恼，爽性在政府大楼外面那堆棕榈树②下待着不走了！

①② 为了更加符合现代读者的阅读习惯，本书将原书中民国时期的英文译名"夏罗"（Charlotte）改为现今通行的译名"夏洛特"；"大树"（cabbage palm）改为"棕榈"。——编者注

自个儿享福！晚风正摇着黑沉沉的叶子，轻轻地在咯嘎作响。好，叫他坐在家里，对着大拇指不管事，眼看一生的事业，在哈罗德秀美的手指缝里溜跑，消散，临了整个儿完事，一面哈罗德在笑……

"爹呀，你为什么不讲理？真是完全地用不着，你天天地到公司去。人家见了你反而笑话你老态，说你神气看得多倦，这不是让我们也不好意思吗？这儿有的是大房子，花园。还不会自个儿享福，单就生活换个样儿，也就有意思不是？要不然你就来一样嗜好，消遣也好。"

洛拉①那孩子就提起嗓子唱了进来，"谁都得有点儿嗜好，要不然就过不了活。"

得，得！他忍不住恶狠狠地笑了，一面他使着狠劲，在爬那小山，过了小山就是哈科特②大路。他要是有了嗜好，夏洛特和洛拉那群孩子，便怎么办？他倒要问问。嗜好付不了房租，付不了海边的避暑，付不了她们的马、她们的高尔夫球戏，付不了她们音乐间里跳舞用六十几磅的传声机。并不是他舍不得她们花费。不，她们全是顶漂亮、顶好看的女孩子，夏洛特也是位了不得的太太，活该她们那么混，真的是，全城里哪一家都比不上他

---

①②　为了更加符合现代读者的阅读习惯，本书将原书中民国时期的英文译名"老腊"（Lola）改为现今通行的译名"洛拉"；"哈各德"（Harcourt）改为"哈科特"。——编者注

们家那么交际广，体面。可不是，老尼夫先生每回在客厅桌上推着烟匣子让客，听的总是好话，称赞他的太太，称赞他的女孩子，甚至称赞他自己。

"你们是个理想的家庭，老先生，一个理想的家庭，仿佛是在书上念到的或是戏台上看的似的。"

"算了算了，我的孩子，"老尼夫先生答道，"试试这烟，看合适不合适？你要愿意到花园去抽烟，孩子们大概全在草地上玩着哪。"

所以这群女孩子全没有嫁人，人家就这么说。她们愿意嫁谁都成，可是她们在家太乐了。她们整天地在一起玩，多么乐，女孩子们外加夏洛特，哼，哼！得了，得了！许是这么回事。……

他已经走完了那条时髦的哈科特大路；他已经到了街角那所屋子，他们的住宅。进出车马的门推在那里；地上有新过的车轮痕迹，他面对着这所白漆的大楼，窗子满开着，花纱的窗帘向外飘着，宽阔的窗沿上摆着风信子①的蓝瓷花盆。车道的两边满开着他们的绣球花②，全城有名的。一穗穗粉红的、浅蓝的花，像阳光似的和杂在纷披的叶子中间，老尼夫先生看看屋子，看看花，又看看车道上新印的轮迹，仿佛他们都在对他说此地有的是

---

①②　为了更加符合现代读者的阅读习惯，本书将原书中民国时期的英译花名"玉簪花"（hyacinth）改为现今通行的译名"风信子"；"紫阳花"（hydrangea）改为"绣球花"。——编者注

青年的生活，有的是女孩子们！

外厅里还是老样子，昏沉沉的满是围巾、洋伞、手套等类，全堆在那橡木柜架上。音乐间里有琴声，又快又响，不耐烦的琴声。客厅的门半掩着，漏出里面的人声。

"那么，有冰淇淋没有呢？"夏洛特的声音，接着她摇椅的嘎吱嘎吱。

"冰淇淋！"埃塞尔叫道，"我的亲娘，你从没有见过那样的冰淇淋，就是两种，一种是平常店里的小草莓①冰，沿边化的全是水。"

"那饭整个坏得太可怕了。"玛丽安接着说。

"可是，冰淇淋总还太早点。"夏洛特缓缓地说。

"怎么呢，要有就得好。"埃塞尔又开口。

"对呀！宝贝。"夏洛特轻着口音说。

忽然音乐间的门啪地打开了，洛拉冲了进来，她一见老尼夫先生站着，吓了一跳，差一点喊了出来。

"啊呵，是爹！你吓得我！你才回家吗？怎么的查尔斯②不来帮你脱外套？"

她满脸通红，两眼发光，头发落在额上，她气喘得像方从

---

①② 为了更加符合现代读者的阅读习惯，本书将原书中民国时期的英文译名"杨梅"(Strawbeny) 改为现今通行的译名"草莓"。"查利士"(Charles) 改为现今通行的译名"查尔斯"。——编者注

暗里跑了出来，受了惊似的，原来这就是洛拉，是不是，但是她似乎把老子忘了；她等在那里可不是为他；她把捏绉了的手绢角放在牙齿中间，恨恨地尽拽着。电话响了。啊啊！洛拉吱的一声叫，当着他的面直冲了过去。嘭的一声电话间的门关紧了，同时夏洛特叫道，"孩子爹，是你不是？"

"你又乏了，"夏洛特抱怨地说着，她停止了她的摇椅，把她暖暖的熟梅似的脸凑上去让他亲吻。

头发铄亮的埃塞尔在他的胡子上啄了一下，玛丽安的口唇刷着他的耳。

"你走回来的，孩子爹？"夏洛特问。

"是，我走回家的。"老尼夫先生说着，在一张客厅大椅里沉了下去。

"可是你为什么不坐个车？"埃塞尔问，"那时候有的是车，要几百都有。"

"我的乖乖埃塞尔，"玛丽安叫道，"要是爹真愿意累坏他自个儿，我看我们也没有法子去干涉。"

"孩子们，孩子们。"夏洛特甜着口音劝着。

玛丽安可不肯停嘴："不，娘，你宠坏了爹，那不对的。你得对他认真点儿，他是顶顽皮。"她笑着她又硬又响的笑，对着镜子掠她的头发。真怪！她小的时候，嗓子顶软，话也说不出口似的，她有时简直是口吃，可是现在，不论说什么——就是在饭桌上的"爹，劳驾，果酱。"——她总是唱着高调，仿佛在台上唱戏似的。

"你来的时候哈罗德离了公司没有，我爱？"

夏洛特问道，又把座椅摇了起来。

"我不很清楚。"老尼夫先生说。

"我说不上，四点钟以后我就没有见他。"

"他说……"夏洛特正要说下去，埃塞尔在报纸里乱翻了一阵，忽然跑过来，蹲在她娘椅子的旁边叫道："这儿，你看，我说的就是那个。妈，黄的，有点银色的，你不爱吗？"

"给我吧！宝贝，"夏洛特说，她摸着了她的玳瑁眼镜，戴上了，把她丰腴的小手指，轻抚着那页纸，把她的口唇荷包似的卷了起来。"呎，真可爱！"她含糊小语着；她从眼镜边儿上面望出来，看看埃塞尔。"我可不喜那裙飘①。"

"不喜那裙飘！"埃塞尔哭丧着声音喊道，"好的就是那裙飘。"

"我来，娘让我看。"玛丽安咄地把那页纸从夏洛特手中抢了过去。"我说娘是对的，"她高兴地喊说，"有了那裙飘，看起来太重了。"

---

① "裙飘"（Train），礼服后背曳地之裙条。——编者注

老尼夫先生，人家早把他忘了，一和身沉在他座椅的宽边儿里面，昏昏地假寐着，听她们说话，仿佛在做梦似的。他真是乏了；他再也使不出劲儿。今夜连自己的太太和女孩子们，他都受不住，她们是太……太……

　　他半睡着地在心里所能想着的就只——他是大富了。在什么事情的背后，他都看见有个枯干的小老头儿在爬着无穷尽的楼梯，他是谁呢？

　　"今晚上我不换衣服了，"他含糊地说。"你说什么，爹？""呃！什么，什么？"老尼夫先生惊醒了，睁着眼向她们望。"我今晚上不换衣服了。"他又说一遍。

　　"可是我们请了露西尔①、达文波特②，还有沃克③太太。"

　　"那可不是春的不大好，一拆样儿。"

　　"你人好过吗，我爱？"

　　"你自己又不用使劲，要查尔斯干什么？"

　　"可是你要真是来不得……"夏洛特在迟疑。

　　"成，成，成。"老尼夫站了起来，自个儿跑上楼，他方才隐约梦见爬楼梯的那个小老头儿，仿佛就在他面前引路。年轻的查尔斯已经在更衣房里等他，很小心的他在拿一块手巾围着那热

---

①②③　为了更加符合现代读者的阅读习惯，本书将原书中民国时期的英文译名"罗雪儿"（Lucile）改为现今通行的译名"露西尔"；"达文伯"（Darenport）改为"达文波特"；"华革"（Walker）改为"沃克"。——编者注

水桶。年轻的查尔斯，自从脸子红红的小孩子时候到家来收拾火炉以来，就是他最爱的当差。老尼夫先生一进房，坐下在窗口一张藤编的长椅上，伸出了一双腿，照例开他每晚的小玩笑。

"查尔斯把他打扮起来了！"查尔斯皱着眉，深深地呼吸着，凑上前去把他领结里的针拔了出来。

呒，呒！好，好！坐在打开的窗前很爽快，很爽快——很温和的黄昏。下面正有人在网球场上剪草，他听到刈草器的咄咄声。不久那女孩子们又要开网球会了。一想着球会，他就好像听到玛丽安的声音荡着，"有你的，伙计……打着了，伙计，啊，真好哪！"接着夏洛特在廊下叫着："哈罗德在哪儿？"埃塞尔说："他总不在这儿，娘。"夏洛特又含糊地回着："他说……"

老尼夫先生叹了一口气，站了起来，一手摸在他胡子的下面，从查尔斯手里取过梳子，很当心地把他白胡子梳了几道，查尔斯递给他一块折齐的手帕，他的表和图章、眼镜盒子。"合适了，孩子。"门关上了，他又坐了下去，就是他一个人……

现在那小老头儿又在下无穷尽的楼梯，来到楼下漂亮的饭厅里，灯火开得旺旺的。

啊！他的腿！像蜘蛛的腿——细小，干瘪了的。

"你们是个理想的家庭。"可是那话要是实，为什么夏洛特或是女孩子们不曾留住他？为什么他老是一个人，爬上爬下的，老是一个人？哈罗德在哪里？啊！再不要盼望哈罗德什么事。下去了，那小小的老蜘蛛下去了。老尼夫先生心里害怕，因为他见他溜过了饭厅，出了门，上了暗沉沉的车道，出了车马进出的门，到了公司。你们留住他，留住他，有人没有！

老尼夫先生又惊觉了。他的更衣房里已经黑了，窗口只有些惨淡的光。他睡了有多久？他听着，他听得远远的人声，远远的声浪，穿过这又高又大昏黑了的房子，传到他的耳边。也许，他昏沉地在想，他已经睡得好久了，谁也没有记着他，全忘他，这屋子、夏洛特、女孩子们、哈罗德——与他有什么相干，他知道他们什么事？他们是他的生人。生命已经在他面前过去了。夏洛特已不是他的妻子，他的妻子！……黑沉沉的门口，一半让情藤给掩着了，情藤仿佛懂得人情，也在垂头丧气，发愁似的。小的暖的手臂绕着他的项颈。一只又小又白的脸，对他仰着，一个口音说道："再会罢，我的宝贝。"

我的宝贝！"再会吧，我的宝贝。"她们里面哪一个说的，她们为什么要再会？准是错了，她是他的妻，那个面色苍白的小女孩子，此外他的一生只是一个梦。

这时候门开了，年轻的查尔斯，站在灯亮里，垂着一双手，像个年轻的兵士，大声喊道："饭已经端出来了，先生！"

"我来了，我来了！"老尼夫先生说。

刮　风

The Wind Blows

忽然间，怪害怕的，她醒了转来。有什么事？出了什么不得了的事似的。不，什么事都没有。就是风，刮着房子，摇着窗，砸响着屋顶上的一块铁皮，连她睡着的床都在直晃。树叶子在窗外乱飞，飞上来，又飞了去。下面马路上飞起一整张的报纸，在半空中直爬，像一只断线风筝，又掉了下去，挂在一株松树上。天冷着哪。夏天完了——这是秋天了——什么都看得寒碜，运货车的铁轮子响着走过，一边一边地摆着；两个中国人肩上扛着安蔬菜筐子的木架子在道上一颠一颠地走着——他们的辫子蓝布衫在风里横着飞。一只白狗跷着一条腿嗥着冲过前门。什么都完事了！什么？喔，全完了！她那手指抖抖地编着她的头发，不敢往镜子里看。娘在厅上给祖母说着话。

"蠢死了！这天色还不把晒着的东西全收了进来……我那块顶精致的小茶桌纱布简直给刮成了破布条儿。那怪味儿是什么呀？麦粥烧焦了。可了不得——这风！"

她十点钟有音乐课。这一想着贝多芬①低半音的调子，就在她的脑子里直转，音波颤动着又长又尖的像是小摇鼓儿。……斯温森②家的玛丽跑到间壁园子里去采菊花省得叫风给白糟蹋了。她的裙子抹上腰身撑开了飞；她想给往下按着，蹲下去把它夹在

---

①② 为了更加符合现代读者的阅读习惯，本书将原书中民国时期的英文译名"贝德花芬"（Beethoven）改为现今通行的译名"贝多芬"。"史"（Swainson）改为现今通行的译名"斯温森"。——编者注

腿中间，可是不成，呼地它还是往上飞。她身旁的树、草，全摇着。她尽快地采，可是她的心乱着。她也顾不得花，随便乱来——把花连根子都起了出来，胡乱地折着揪着，顿着脚赌咒。

"你们就不会把前门关上！绕到背后去关。"有人在嚷着。接着她听见宝健："娘，找你说电话。电话，娘。肉铺子的。"

这日子多难过——烦死，真叫人烦……得，这回她帽子上的宽紧带又炸了。不炸还怎么着。她换上了一顶旧软帽，想走后门溜出去。可是娘已经见了。

"玛蒂尔达^①，玛蒂尔达。快——快快地回来！怎么着你头上戴的是什么呀？倒像个盖茶壶的软兜子。那一纠长头发又给甩在前面算什么了。"

"我不进来了，娘。我上课去，已经太迟了。"

"赶快回来！"

她不。她不干。她恨娘。"去你的。"她大声叫着，往街上直跑。

海里浪似的，天上云似的，一卷卷大圆股儿的土直迎着来刺人，土里还夹着一点点的稻草、米糠、焙干的肥料。园子里的树大声地叫着，她站在路尽头布伦^②先生的家门前，连海的啸

---

①② 为了更加符合现代读者的阅读习惯，本书将原书中民国时期的英文译名"玛提达"（Matilda）改为现今通行的译名"玛蒂尔达"。"普伦"（Bullen）改为"布伦"。——编者注

响都听着了："啊！……啊！……啊！啊！"但是布伦先生的客厅里还是山洞一样的静。窗子全关着，窗幔拉下一半，她并没来晚。"在她前面的那女孩子"正练着麦克道威尔的《冰岛歌》。布伦先生转眼过来看着她，半笑不笑的。

"坐下，"他说。"坐那边那个沙发，小姑娘。"

多怪，他那样儿。也不能说他一定怎么笑你……可是总有点儿……这屋子里多清静呀。她喜欢这间屋子，闻着有毛哔叽、陈烟、菊花的味儿……火炉架上鲁宾斯坦①那相片的背后放着一大盆那……"送给我的好友罗伯特·布伦②"……那黑色闪光的钢琴上也挂着"孤独"——一个穿白衣服脸上暗沉沉神情悲惨的妇人，坐在一块石头上，她的腿交叠着，她的下巴在她的手上。

"不，不！"布伦先生说，他就靠下身子去，把他的胳膊放在那女孩子的肩膀上，替她弹了一道。这笨劲——她面红了！多可笑！

在她前面的那女孩子走了；前门嘭地关上了。布伦先生回进房来，来回地走着，他那温和的样子，等着她。这事情多怪呀。她的手指儿直发震，连那音乐书包上的结子都解不下来。这是风刮的……她的心也直跳，仿佛她那裙子准叫风刮得一上一下地乱

---

①② 为了更加符合现代读者的阅读习惯，本书将原书中民国时期的英文译名"鲁本斯达"（Rubinstein）改为现今通行的译名"鲁宾斯坦"；"洛勃普伦"（Robert Bullen）改为"罗伯特·布伦"。——编者注

飞。布伦先生一句话也不说。那张旧的红绒琴凳子长够两个人并着坐。布伦先生并着她坐下了。

"我先试试指法好不好？"她问，捧着一双手紧紧地挤。"我也练过一点快指法。"

但是他不回话。竟许他听都没有听见……忽然间他的白净的手戴着一个戒指的伸了过来，打开了贝多芬。

"我们稍微来一点大家的吧。"他说。

但是为什么他说话这样的和气——这太和气——倒像他们是老朋友，彼此什么都明白似的。

他慢慢地翻着书篇。她看着他的手——多美的一只手，看得老像是才洗干净似的。

"有了。"布伦先生说。

啊，他那和气的声音——啊，那低半音的调子。这是小鼓声来了……

"我来试一遍好不好？"

"好，好孩子。"

他的声音是太，太过分的和气了。那乐谱上的半音符与快半音符直跳着像是一群黑小孩子在墙篱上跳着玩似的。他为什么这……她不哭——她没有什么要哭的……

"怎么了，好孩子？"

布伦先生拿了她的手。他的肩膀正挨着她的头。她就这一点点儿靠着它，她的脸挨着那疏松的粗呢。

"做人没有意思。"她低声地说，可是她一点也不觉得没有意思。他也说了些什么"等一等"，"小心拍板"，"那珍贵的东西，一个女人"，但是她没有听着。这多舒服……老是这……

突然间门开了，斯温森家的玛丽窜了进来，离她的时候还远着远着哪。

"这快调还得快一点。"布伦先生说，他站了起来，又在屋子里来回地走着。

"坐那沙发椅，小姑娘。"他对玛丽说。

这风，这风。一个人坐在她自个儿屋子里怪害怕的。那床，那镜子，那脸盆小壶，全亮着，像外面的天。这张床就叫人怕。它躺在那里，睡得着着的……娘得知不得知这被盖上放着一纠纠像蛇盘似的袜子全得我补？她再不想。不，娘。我不知道为什么，我一定得……这风，这风！烟囱里刮下来有煤灰味儿。有谁写诗给风的？……"我带花给叶子给雨。"……胡扯。

"是你呀，宝健？"

"来同我到海边上去走走，玛蒂尔达。这我再也受不住了。"

"有理。让我披上外套。这天多坏！"宝健的外套跟她的一样。扣上了领子她对镜子里照了照自己。她脸是白的，他们俩一样有那火亮的眼，火热的嘴。啊，镜子里的一对他们认识。再见，乖乖；我们就回来的。

"这样好，是不是？"

"扣上了。"宝健说。

他们走得总不够快。低着头，腿正碰着，他们俩看是一个急忙忙的人，走完大街，走下那长满着小茴香花的不整齐的沥青道，从这下去就是靠海那块平地。天晚了——正是黄昏时。大风刮得他们俩走都走不稳，冲着风左颠右跛的像一对酒醉鬼。大场上的野草花儿全叫风给吹倒了。

"来呀！来呀！我们走近一点。"

过了那堤防，外面的海里浪起得顶高。他们脱了帽子，她的头发吹进她的嘴里，满是盐味儿，海里风太大了，浪头直往上鼓，也不开花；浪上来嗤嗤地打着堤防的大石壁，长草的滴水的石级全叫淹了去。一股劲浪直冲了过来。他们身上全是水点；她的嘴里尝着又湿又凉的。

宝健说着话哪。他说话的声音一高一低的。顶怪的——听了可笑——可是那天正合适。风带着他们的声音—— 一句句话直往外飞，像是一条条小的窄的丝带。

"快一点！快一点！"

天愈迟愈黑了。海湾里上煤的靠船上有两个灯—— 一个高高地在桅上，一个在船艄上。

"看，宝健。看那边。"

一只大的黑轮船冒着一大卷烟，船舱圆窗洞里全默着亮，船上那处全是亮，正在开出去。大风留不住她；她破着浪走，向着那两边是光石子的湾门口去，这去是到……就这光过来显得她异样，又美又神秘的……他们俩臂挽臂地在船阑上靠着哪。

"……他们是谁？"

"弟弟跟姊。"

"看，宝健，那是我们的镇。看得真小不是？那是最末了一次的邮局钟。那是那块大场地那天大风天我们在走着的。你记得不？那天我上音乐课还哭哪——多少年前的事！再会吧，小岛，再会……"

这忽见黑夜伸出一个翅膀盖住了沸翻的海水。他们瞧不见他们俩了。再会，再会。别忘了……但是那船已经走了！这时候。

附录一

夜深时（残篇）

……①

抓不到，你干着急也没有用，谁都盼望总攻击时那一阵的浓味儿，出了性拼命时有神仙似的快乐，但谁都摸不准总司令先生的脾胃，大家等着那一天，那一天可偏是慢吞吞地不到。

宕着，悬着，挂着，永不生根，什么事都是像我们的地球一样，滚是滚着，可没有进步，男的与女的：好像是最亲密不过，最亲热不过，最亲昵不过的是两口子不是？可是事情没有这样简单，他们中间隔着的道儿正长着呢！你是站在纽约五十八层的高楼上望着，她在吴淞炮台那里瞭着，你们的镜头永远对不准。

不准才有意思，才有意思。愈看不准，你愈要想对，愈晃着镜子对，愈没有准儿，可是这里面就是生活，悲剧，趣剧，哈哈，眼泪，文学，艺术，人生观，大学教授，京报附刊，全是一个网里捞出来的鱼。

我说的话，你摸不清理路不是？原要你摸不清，谁要你摸得清？你摸得清，就没有我的落儿！

十九世纪出了一个圣人，他现在还活着。圣人！谁是圣人，什么圣人？不忙，我记得口袋里有的是定义，让我看看。"圣人就是他"——这外国句法不成，你须得轮头来。谁要能说一句话或一篇话，只要他那里有一部分人想得到可是说不上的道德，他

就是圣人。"我未见好德如好色者也"，那是孔二爷。这话说得顶平常，顶不出奇，谁都懂得，谁都点头儿说对。好比你说猫鼻子没有狗鼻子长，顶对，这就是圣。圣人的话永远平常的，一出世他也许是一个吴稚晖，或是谁，那也不坏，可就不是圣人。

可是我说的现代的圣人又是谁？他有两个名字：在外国叫勃那萧，在中国叫萧伯纳。他为什么是圣人？他写了一本戏，谁都知道的叫做《人与超人》。一篇顶长，顶繁，顶啰唆的戏，前面还装着一篇一样长，繁，啰唆的长序。但是他说的就是一句话，证明的就是一句话；这话就是——凡是男与女发生关系时，女的永远是追的那个，男的永远是躲的那个，这话可没有我孔二爷的老实，不错，分别是有，东洋孔二爷是戴平天冠，捧着白玉圭，头顶朝着天，脚跟踏着地，眼睛看着鼻子，鼻子顾着胡子，大胡子挂在心坎上，条理分明地轻易不得吹糊。他们的萧伯纳是满脸长着细白毛，像是龙井茶的毛尖，他自己说是叫虫子啃过的草地，他的站法顶别致，他的不是 A 字式的站法，他的是 Y 字式的站法，他不叫他的腿站在地上，那太平常不出奇，他叫他的脑袋支着地，有时一双手都不去帮忙，两条腿直挺挺地开着顶对天花板，为是难为了他的颈根酸了一点，他这三四十年来就是玩着这把戏——一块朝天马蹄铁的思想家，一个"拿大顶"的圣人。这分别你就看出来了不是？用腿的站得住（那也不容易有人到几十岁还摔跤呢），用头的也站住了，也许萧先生比孔先生觉得累一点，可是他的好看多了；这一来他们说话的道儿就不同，一是顺着来的，一是反着来的，反正他们一样说得回老家就是——真理是他们的老家。

孔二爷理想中的社会是拿几条粗得怕人的大绳子拴得稳稳的社会，尤其是男与女的中间放着一座掀不动钻不透的"大防"。孔二爷看事情真不含糊，黄就是黄，青就是青，男就是男，女就是女，干脆，男女是危险的。你简直要想法子，要不然就出乱子。你得防着他们，真的你得防着他们，把野兽装进了铁笼子，随他多凶猛也得屈服。别的不必说，就是公公媳妇大伯弟妇都得要防防，哥哥妹妹弟弟姊姊都得要防防，六岁以上就不准同桌子吃饭，夫妇也不准过分地亲近：老爷进了房，太太来了一个客人，家里来了外人，太太爱张张也得躲到屏风背后去。这样不但女子没法子找男子，就是男子也不得机会去找女子了。结果防范愈严，危险愈大，所以每回一闹乱子我们就益发地佩服孔二爷的见解高明。不错，这野兽其实也太不讲礼，太猖獗，只有用粗索子去拴住他，拿铁笼子去关住他，我从不反过头来想想——假如把所有的绳子全放宽，把一切的笼子全打开了，看这一大群的野畜生又打什么主意。

萧伯纳的回答说不碍，随你放得怎样宽，人类总是不会灭的；废弃了一切人为的法律；逃避了一切人群的势力，我们还是躲不了生命的势力（Life force）。男人着忙去找女人，或是女人着忙去带着一个男人；这就是潜在的生命的势力活动的证据。男人的事务是去寻饭吃，女人的事务是生殖；男人的作用是经济的，女人的作用是生物的。女人天生有极强极牢固的母性；她为要完成她的天职，她就（也许不觉得地）想望生活的固定，顶要紧是有一个家。但是男人却往往怕难，自己寻食吃已经够难，替一家寻食吃当然更是麻烦；他有时还存心躲懒；实际上他怕的是一个永久固定的家。还有一个理由为什么女人比男人更着急，那是因为女性美是不久长的，她的引诱力是暂时而且有限的，所以她得赶紧；一个女儿过了三十岁还不出嫁父母就急，连亲戚都替她担忧。其实她自己又何尝不急，只是在老社会情况底下她没有机会表示意志就是。她急的缘故也不完全是为要得男人的爱，她着急是为要完成她的职务，为要满足她的母性。所以萧伯纳是不错的，他说在一个选择自由的社会里男女间有关系发生时，女的往往是追的那个，男的倒反是躲的那个。王尔德说男子总不愿意结婚除非他是厌倦了，女子结婚为的是好奇。这话至少一半是对的，平常一个有志气爱自由的男子哪肯轻易去冒终身企业的危险？去担负养活一个家的仔肩？反面说女人倒是常常在心里打算的（她们很少肯认账，竟许也有自己不感觉到的，但实际却有这种情形），打算她身世的寄托，打算她将来的家，打算亲手替她亲生子打小鞋做小袜子。并不是女子的羞耻，这正是她的荣耀。这是她对人道的义务。要是有一天理性的发展竟然消灭了这点子本性，人类种族的生产与生存也就成了问题了。我们不盼望有那一天，虽则我们看了"理性的"或是"智理的"的女人一天一天增加数目，有远虑的就多少不免担忧。

曼殊斐尔是个心理的写实派，她不仅写实，她简直是写真。你要是肯下相当的工夫去读懂她的作品，你才相信她是天才无可疑的；她至少是二十世纪最重要的作者的一个，她的字一个个都是活的，一个个都是有意义的，在她最精粹的作品里我们简直不能增也不能减，更不能更动她一个字；随你怎样奥妙的细微的曲折的，有时刻薄的心理她都有恰好的法子来表现；她手里擒住的不是一个个的字，是人的心灵变化的真实，一点也不错了。法国一个画家叫德加①（Degas）能捉住电光下舞女银色的衣裳急旋时的色彩与情调；曼殊斐尔，也能分析出电光似急射飞跳的神经作用；她的艺术，（仿佛是高尔斯华绥说的）是在时间与空间的缝道里下功夫，她的方法不是用镜子反映，不用笔白描，更不是从容幻想，她分明是伸出两个不容情的指头，到人的脑筋里

---

① 原文为"台迦"（Degas），现通译为"德加"（1834~1917），法国画家。——编者注

去生生地捉住成形不露面的思想的影子，逼住他们现原形！短篇小说到了她的手里，像契诃夫^①（她唯一的老师）的手里，才是纯粹的美术（不止是艺术）；她斫成的玉是不仅没有疤癜，不沾土灰，她的都是成品的，最高的艺术是形式与本质（Form and Substance）化成一体再也分不开的妙制；我们看曼殊斐尔的小说就分不清哪里是式，哪里是质，我们所得的只是一个印象，一个真的、美的印象，仿佛是在冷静的溪水里看横斜的梅花的影子，清切，神妙，美。

这篇《夜深时》并不是她最高的作品，但我们多少可以领略她特别的意味，她写一段心理是很普通的很不出奇的；一个快上年纪的独身女子着急找一个男人；她看上了一个，她写信给他，送袜子给他；碰一个冷钉子；这回晚上独自坐在火炉前冥想，羞，恨，怨，自怜，急，自慰，悸，自伤，想丢，丢不下；想抛，抛不了；结果爬上床去蒙紧被窝淌眼泪哭，她是谁，我们不必问，我们只知道她是一个近人情的女子；她在白天做什么事，明天早起说什么话，我们全不必管，我们有特权窃听的就是她今夜上单个儿坐在渐灭的炉火前的一番心境，一段自诉，她并不说出口，但我们仿佛亲耳听着她说话，一个字也不含糊。也许有人说损，这一挖苦女人太厉害了，但我们应

---

① 原文为"柴霍甫"，现通译为"契诃夫"（1860～1904），俄国小说家、戏剧家。——编者注

问的是她写得真不真，只要真就满足了艺术的条件，损不损是另外一件事。

乘便我们在这篇里也可以看出萧伯纳的"女追男躲"的一个解释。这当然也可以当做弗洛伊德的心理学的注解者，但我觉得陪衬"萧"更有趣些，所以南天北海地胡扯了这一长篇，告罪告罪！

附录二

曼殊斐尔

这心灵深处的欢畅，

这情绪境界的壮旷；

任天堂沉沦，地狱开放，

毁不了我内府的宝藏！

——康河晚照即景

美感的记忆，是人生最可珍的产业。认识美的本能，是上帝给我们进天堂的一把密钥。

有人的性情，例如我自己的，如以气候作喻，不但是阴晴相间，而且常有狂风暴雨，也有最艳丽蓬勃的春光。有时遭逢幻灭，引起厌世的悲观，铅般的重压在心上，比如冬令阴霾，到处冰结，莫有些微生气；那时便怀疑一切：宇宙、人生、自我，都只是幻的妄的；人情、希望、理想，也只是妄的幻的。

Ah, human nature, how,

If utterly frail thou art and vile,

If dust thou art and ashes, is thy heart so great?

If thou art noblo in part,

How are thy loftiest and impulses and thoughts

By so ignoble causes kindled and put out

"Sopra un ritratto di una bella donna"

这几行是最深入的悲观派诗人莱奥帕尔迪[①]（Leopardi）的诗。一座荒坟的墓碑上，刻着冢中人生前美丽的肖像，激起了他这根本的疑问——若说人生是有理可寻的，何以到处只是矛盾的现象，若说美是幻的，何以他引起的心灵反动能有如此之深切，若说美是真的，何以也可以与常物同归腐朽，但莱奥帕尔迪探海灯似的智力虽则把人间种种事物虚幻的外像，一一给褫剥了，连宗教都剥成了个赤裸的梦，他却没有力量来否认美！美的创现他只能认为是称奇的，他也不能否认高洁的精神恋，虽则他不信女子也能有同样的境界。在感美感恋最纯粹的一刹那间，莱奥帕尔迪不能不承认是极乐天国的消息，不能不承认是生命中最宝贵的经验。所以我每次无聊到极点的时候，在层冰般严封的心河底里，突然涌起一股消融一切的热流，顷刻间消融了厌世的结晶，消融了烦闷的苦冻。那热流便是感美感恋最纯粹的一俄顷之回忆。

[①] 原文为"理巴第"（Leopardi），现通译为"莱奥帕尔迪"（1793~1837），意大利诗人。——编者注

To see a world in a grain of sand,

And a Heaven in a wild flower,

Hold Infinity in the palm of your hand,

And eternity in an hour.

从一颗沙里看出世界，

天堂的消息在一朵野花，

将无限存在你的掌上。

刹那间有无穷的边涯……

这类神秘性的感觉，当然不是普遍的经验，也不是常有的经验，凡事只讲实际的人，当然嘲讽神秘主义，当然不能相信科学可解释的神经作用，会发生科学所不能解释的神秘感觉，但世上"可为知者道不可与不知者言"的情事正多着呢！

从前在十六世纪，有一次有一个意大利的牧师学者到英国乡下去，见了一大片盛开的苜蓿（clover）在阳光中只似一湖欢舞的黄金。他只惊喜得手足无措，慌忙跪在地上，仰天祷告，感谢上帝的恩典，使他见得这样的美，这样的神景。他这样发疯似的举动，当时一定招起在旁乡下人的哗笑。我这篇要讲的经历，恐怕也有些那牧师狂喜的疯态，但我也深信读者里自有同情的人，所以我也不怕遭乡下人的笑话！

去年七月中有一天晚上，天雨地湿，我独自冒着雨在伦敦的汉普斯特德（Hampstead）问路警，问行人，在寻邦德街第十号的屋子。那就是我初次，不幸也是末次，会见曼殊斐尔——"那二十分不死的时间！"——的一晚。

我先认识默里①君（John Middleton Murry），他是 *Atheneaum* 的总主笔，诗人，著名评论家，也是曼殊斐尔一生最后十余年间最密切的伴侣。

他和她自一九一三年起，即夫妇相处，但曼殊斐尔却始终用她到英国以后的"笔名"Katharine Mansfield。她生长于新西兰②（New Zealand），原名是 Kathleen Beanchamp，是新西兰银行经理 Sir Harold Beanchamp 的女儿。她十五年前离开了本乡，同着三个小妹子到英国，进伦敦大学皇后学院读书。她从小就以美慧著名，但身体也从小即很怯弱。她曾在德国住过，那时她写她的第一本小说 "*In a German Pension*"。大战期间她在法国的时候多。近几年她也常在瑞典、意大利及法国南部。她常住外国，就为她身体太弱，禁不得英伦雾迷雨苦的天时，默里为了伴她，也只得把一部分的事业放弃，（"*Atheneaum*"之所以并入"*London Nation*"就为此。）跟着他安琪儿似的爱妻，寻求健康。据说可

---

① 原文为"麦雷"（John Middleton Murry），通译为"约翰·米德尔顿·默里"（1889～1957），英国作家。——编者注
② 原文为"纽新兰"（New Zealamd），通译为"新西兰"。——编者注

怜的曼殊斐尔战后得了肺病，证明以后，医生明说她不过两三年的寿限，所以默里和她相处有限的光阴，真是分秒可数。多见一次夕照，多经一次朝旭，她优昙似的余荣，便也消减了如许的活力，这颇使人想起茶花女一面吐血一面纵酒恣欢时的名句："You know I have not long to live, therefore *I will live fast*!"——你知道我是活不久长的，所以我存心活他一个痛快！

我正不知道多情的默里，眼看这艳丽无双的夕阳，渐渐消翳，心里"爱莫能助"的悲感，浓烈到何等田地！

但曼殊斐尔的"活他一个痛快"的方法，却不是像茶花女的纵酒恣欢，而是在文艺中努力。她像夏夜榆林中的鹃鸟，呕出缕缕的心血来制成无双的情曲，即便唱到血枯音嘶，也还不忘她的责任是牺牲自己有限的精力，替自然界多增几分的美，给苦闷的人间几分艺术化精神的安慰。

她心血所凝成的便是两本小说集，一本是"*Bliss*"，一本是去年出版的"*Garden Party*"。凭这两部书里的二三十篇小说，她已经在英国的文学界里占了一个很稳固的位置。一般的小说只是小说，她的小说是纯粹的文学，真的艺术；平常的作者只求暂时的流行，博群众的欢迎，她却只想留下几小块"时灰"掩不暗的真晶，只要得少数知音者的赞赏。

但唯其是纯粹的文学，她的著作的光彩是深蕴于内而不是显露于外的，其趣味也须读者用心咀嚼，方能充分地理会。我承作者当面许可选译她的精品，如今她去世，我更应当珍重实行我翻译的特权，虽则我颇怀疑我自己的胜任。我的好友陈通伯所知道的欧洲文学恐怕在北京比谁都更渊博些，他在北大教短篇小说，曾经讲过曼殊斐尔的，这很使我欢喜。他现在也答应也来选译几篇，我更要感谢他了。关于她短篇艺术的长处，我也希望通伯能有机会说一点。

现在让我讲那晚怎样地会晤曼殊斐尔。早几天我和默里在Charing Cross 背后一家嘈杂的A. B. C. 茶店里，讨论英法文坛的状况，我乘便说起近几年中国文艺复兴的趋向，在小说里感受俄国作者的影响最深，他喜得几乎跳了起来，因为他们夫妻最崇拜俄国的几位大家，他曾经特别研究过陀思妥耶夫斯基①，著有一本 "Dastoievsky: A Critical Study"，曼殊斐尔又是私淑契诃夫②（Tchekhov）的，他们常在抱憾俄国文学始终不曾受英国人相当的注意，因之小说的质与式，还脱不尽维多利亚时期的Philistinism（即庸俗主义）。我又乘便问起曼殊斐尔的近况，他说她一时身体颇过得去，所以此次敢伴着她回伦敦住两星期，他就给了我他们的住址，请我星期四晚上去会她和他们的朋友。

①② 原文为"道施滔庵符斯基"（Dastoievsky），通译为"陀思妥耶夫斯基"（1821～1881），俄国作家。原文为"契诃甫"（Tchekhov），通译为"契诃夫"（1860～1904），俄国作家。——编者注

所以我会见曼殊斐尔，真算是凑巧的凑巧。星期三那天我到威尔斯①（H. G. Wells）乡里的家去了（Easten Glebe），下一天和他的夫人一同回伦敦，那天雨下得很大，我记得回寓时浑身全淋湿了。

他们在邦德街的寓处，很不容易找（伦敦寻地方总是麻烦的，我恨极了那回街曲巷的伦敦。），后来居然寻着了，一家小小一楼一底的屋子，默里出来替我开门，我颇狼狈地拿着雨伞，还拿着一个朋友还我的几卷中国字画。进了门，我脱了雨具，他让我进右首一间屋子，我到那时为止对于曼殊斐尔只是对于一个有名的年轻女子作者的景仰与期望；至于她的"仙姿灵态"我那时绝对没有想到，我以为她只是与 Rose Macaulay，Virginia Woolf，Roma Wilson，Vanessa Bell 几位女文学家的同流人物。平常男子文学家与美术家，已经尽够怪僻，近代女子文学家更似乎故意养成怪僻的习惯。最显著的一个通习是装饰之务淡朴，务不入时，务"背女性"：头发是剪了的，又不好好地收拾，一团合糟地散在肩上；袜子永远是粗纱的；鞋上不是沾有泥就是带灰，并且大都是最难看的样式；裙子不是异样的短就是过分的长，眉目间也许有一两圈"天才的黄晕"，或是带着最可厌的美国式龟壳大眼镜，但她们的脸上却从不见脂粉的痕迹，手上装饰亦是永

① 原文为"惠尔斯"（H. G. Wells），通译为"威尔斯"（1866～1946），英国作家。——编者注

远没有的，至多无非是多烧了香烟的焦痕；哗笑的声音，十次有九次半盖过同座的男子；走起路来也是挺胸凸肚的，再也辨不出是夏娃的后身；开起口来大半是男子不敢出口的话；当然最喜欢讨论是 Freudian Complex，Birth Control，或是 George Moore 与 James Joyce 私人印行的新书，例如 "*A Storyteller's Holiday*" 与 "*Ulysses*"。总之，她们的全人格只是一幅妇女解放的讽刺画（Amy Lowell 听说整天地抽大雪茄！）；和这一班立意反对上帝造人的本意的"唯智的"女子在一起，当然也有许多有趣味的地方，但有时总不免感觉她们矫揉造作的痕迹过深，引起一种性的憎忌。

我当时未见曼殊斐尔以前，固然没有想她是这样一流的 Futuristic，但也绝对没有梦想到她是女性的理想化。

所以我推进那门时我就盼望她—— 一个将近中年和蔼的妇人——笑盈盈地从壁炉前沙发上站起来和我握手问安。

但房里—— 一间狭长的壁炉对门的房——只见鹅黄色恬静的灯光，壁上炉架上杂色的美术的陈设和画件，几张有彩色画套的沙发同列在炉前，却没有一半个人影。默里让我一张椅上坐了，伴着我谈天，谈的是东方的观音和基督教的圣母，希腊的 Virgin Diana，埃及的 Isis，波斯的 Mithraism 里的 Virgin 等等之相仿佛，似乎处女的圣母是所有宗教里一个不可少的象征……我们正讲着，只听门上一声剥啄，接着进来了一位年轻的女郎，含笑着站在门口。"难道她就是曼殊斐尔——这样的年轻……"我心里在疑惑，她一头的褐色鬌发，盖着一张小圆脸，眼极活泼，口也很灵动，配着一身极鲜艳的衣装——漆鞋，绿丝长袜，银红绸的上衣，酱紫的丝绒裙——亭亭地立着，像一棵临风的郁金香。

默里起来替我介绍，我才知道她不是曼殊斐尔，而是屋主人，不知是密司B——什么，我记不清了，默里是暂寓在她家的；她是个画家，壁上挂的画，大都是她自己的作品。她在我对面的椅子上坐了。她从炉架上取下一个小发电机似的东西拿在手里，头上又戴了一个接电话生戴的听箍，向我凑得很近地说话，我先还当是无线电的玩具，随后方知这位秀美的女郎的听觉是有缺陷的！

她正坐定，外面的门铃大响——我疑心她的门铃是特别响些。来的是我在弗赖①先生（Roger Fry）家里会过的 Sydney Waterloo，极诙谐的一位先生，有一次他从巨大的口袋里一连掏出了七八支的烟斗，大的小的长的短的，各种颜色的，叫我们好笑。他进来就问默里，凯瑟琳②今天怎样，我竖了耳朵听他的回

---

① 原文为"法兰"（Roger Fry），通译为"罗杰·弗赖"（1866～1934），英国画家、艺术评论家。——编者注
② 原文为"迦赛林"（Katherine），通译为"凯瑟琳"，即曼斯菲尔德的名。——编者注

答。默里说："她今天不下楼了，天气太坏，谁都不受用……"华德鲁先生就问他可否上楼去看她，默里说可以的。华又问了密司B的允许站了起来，他正要走出门，默里又赶过去轻轻地说"Sydney，don't talk too much！"

楼上微微听得步响，W 已在凯瑟琳房中了。一面又来了两个客，一个短的M才从游希腊回来，一个轩昂的美丈夫，就是"*London Nation and Atheneaum*"里每周做科学文章署名 S 的 Sullivan。M 就讲他游历希腊的情形，尽背着古希腊的史迹名胜，Parnassus长，Mycenae 短，讲个不住。S 也问默里凯瑟琳如何，默里说今晚不下楼，W 现在楼上。过了半点钟模样，W 笨重的足音下来了，S 问他凯瑟琳倦了没有，W 说："不，不像倦，可是我也说不上，我怕她累，所以我下来了。"再等一歇，S 也问了默里的允许上楼去，默里也照样叮咛他不要让她乏了。默里问我中国的书画，我乘便就拿那晚带去的一幅赵之谦的"草书法画梅"、一幅王觉斯的草书、一幅梁山舟的行书，打开给他们看，讲了些书法大意，密司 B 听得高兴，手捧着她的听盘，挨近我身旁坐着。

但我那时心里却颇觉失望，因为冒着雨存心要来一会"*Bliss*"的作者，偏偏她不下楼，同时 W、S、默里的烘云托月，又增了我对她的好奇心。我想运气不好，凯瑟琳在楼上，老朋友还有进房去谈的特权，我外国人的生客，一定是没有份的了。时已十时过半了，我只得起身告别，走出房门，默里陪出来帮我穿雨衣。我一面穿衣，一面说我很抱歉，今晚密司曼殊斐尔不能下来，否则我是很想望会她一面的，不意默里竟很诚恳地说："如其你不介意，不妨请上楼去一见。"我听了这话喜出望外，立即将雨衣脱下，跟着默里一步一步地走上楼梯……

上了楼梯，叩门，进房，介绍，S 告辞，和 M 一同出房，关门，她请我坐下，我坐下，她也坐下……这么一大串繁复的手续我只觉得是像电火似的一扯过，其实我只推想应有这么些的经过，却并不曾觉到：当时只觉得一阵模糊。事后每次回想也只觉得是一阵模糊，我们平常从黑暗的街上走进一间灯烛辉煌的屋子，或是从光薄的屋子里出来骤然对着盛烈的阳光，往往觉得耀光太强，头晕目眩的，得定一定神，方能辨认眼前的事物。用英文说就是Senses overwhelmed by excessive light；不仅是光，浓烈的颜色有时也有"潮没"官觉的效能。我想我那时，虽不定是被曼殊斐尔人格的烈光所潮没，她房里的灯光陈设以及她自身衣饰种种各品浓艳灿烂的颜色，已够使我不预防的神经，感觉刹那间的淆惑，那是很可理解的。

她的房给我的印象并不清切，因为她和我谈话时，不容我去认记房中的布置，我只知道房是很小，一张大床差不多就占了全房大部分的地位，壁是用画纸裱的，挂着好几幅油画大概也是主人画的。她和我同坐在床左贴壁一张沙发榻上，因为我斜倚她正坐的缘故，她似乎比我高得多（在她面前哪一个不是低的，真是！）。我疑心那两盏电灯是用红色罩的，否则何以我想起那房，便联想起"红烛高烧"的景象？但背景究属不甚重要，重要的是给我最纯粹的美感的——The purest aesthetic feeling——她；是使我使用上帝给我那把进天国的密钥的——她；是使我灵魂的内府里，又增加了一部宝藏的——她。但要用不驯服的文字来描写那晚的她！不要说显示她人格的精华，就是单只忠实地表现我当时的单纯感象，恐怕就够难的了。从前一个人有一次做梦，进天堂去玩了，他异样的欢喜，明天一起身就到他朋友那里去，想描写他神妙不过的梦境，但是！他站在朋友面前，结住舌头，一个字都说不出来，因为他要说的时候，才觉得他所学的在人间适用的字句，绝对不能表现他梦里所见天堂的景色，他气得从此不开口，后来抑郁而死。我此时妄想用字来活现出一个曼殊斐尔，也差不多有同样的感觉，但我却宁可冒亵渎神灵的罪，免得像那位诚实君子活活地闷死。她的打扮与她的朋友 B 女士相像，也是铄亮的漆皮鞋，闪色的绿丝袜，枣红丝绒的围裙，嫩黄薄绸的上衣，领口是尖开的，胸前挂着一串细珍珠，袖口只齐及肘弯。她的发是黑的，也同密司 B 一样剪短的，但她栉发的样式，却是我在欧美从没有见过的。我疑心她是有心仿效中国式，因为她的发不但纯黑，而且直而不鬈，整整齐齐的一圈，前面像我们十余年前的"刘海"，梳得光滑异常；我虽则说不出所以然，但觉得她发之美也是生平所仅见。

至于她眉目口鼻之清之秀之明净，我其实不能传神于万一；仿佛你对着自然界的杰作，不论是秋水洗净的湖山，霞彩纷披的夕照，或是南洋莹彻的星空，或是艺术界的杰作，贝多芬的交响乐①，瓦格纳②的歌剧③，米开朗琪罗④的雕像，惠斯勒⑤（Whistler）或是柯罗（Corot）的画；你只觉得他们整体的美，纯粹的美，完全的美，不能分析的美，可感不可说的美；你仿佛直接无碍地领会了造化最高明的意志，你在最伟大深刻的戟刺中经验了无限的欢喜，在更大的人格中解化了你的性灵。我看了曼殊斐尔像印度最纯澈的碧玉似的容貌，受着她充满了灵魂的电流的凝视，感着她最和软的春风似的神态，所得的总量我只能称之为一整个的美感。她仿佛是个透明体，你只感讶她粹极的灵彻性，却看不见一些杂质。就是她一身的艳服，如其别人穿着，也

① 原文为"沁芳南"，是"交响乐"（Sinfonia）的音译。——编者注
② 原文为"怀格纳"，通译为"瓦格纳"（1813～1883），德国作曲家。——编者注
③ 原文为"奥配拉"，是"歌剧"（Opera）的音译。——编者注
④ 原文为"密克朗其罗"，通译为"米开朗琪罗"（1834～1903），意大利雕像家、画家。——编者注
⑤ 原文为"卫师德拉"（Whistler），通译为"惠斯勒"（1834～1903），美国画家。——编者注

许会引起琐碎的批评，但在她身上，你只是觉得妥帖，像牡丹的绿叶，只是不可少的衬托。汤林生（H. M. Tomlingson），她生前的一个好友，以阿尔帕斯山巅万古不融的雪，来比拟她清极超俗的美，我以为很有意味的。他说：——

　　曼殊斐尔以美称，然美固未足以状其真，世以可人为美，曼殊斐尔固可人矣，然何其脱尽尘寰气，一若高山琼雪，清彻重霄，其美可惊，而其凉亦可感。艳阳被雪，幻成异彩，亦明明可识，然亦似神境在远，不隶人间。曼殊斐尔肌肤明皙如纯牙，其官之秀，其目之黑，其颊之腴，其约发环整如鬃，其神态之闲静，有华族桀者之明粹，而无西艳伉杰之容；其躯体尤苗约，绰如也，若明蜡之静焰，若晨星之淡妙，就语者未尝不自讶其吐息之重浊，而虑是静且淡者之且神化……

　　汤林生又说她锐敏的目光，似乎直接透入你的灵府深处，将你所蕴藏的秘密，一齐照彻，所以他说她有鬼气，有仙气。她对着你看，不是见你的面之表，而是见你心之底，但她却不是侦刺你的内蕴，不是有目的的搜罗，而只是同情的体贴。你在她面前，自然会感觉对她无慎密的必要；你不说她也有数，你说了她不会惊讶。她不会责备，她不会怂恿，她不会奖赞，她不会代你出什么物质利益的主意，她只是默默地听，听完了然后对你讲她自己超于善恶的见解——真理。

这一段从长期的交谊中出来深入的话，我与她仅仅一二十分钟的接近当然不会体会到，但我敢说从她神灵的目光里推测起来，这几句话不但是可能，而且是极近情的。

所以我那晚和她同坐在蓝丝绒的榻上，幽静的灯光，轻笼住她美妙的全体，我像受了催眠似的，只是痴对她神灵的妙眼，一任她利剑似的光波，妙乐似的音浪，狂潮骤雨似的向我灵府泼淹。我那时即使有自觉的感觉，也只似济慈[①]（Keats）听鹃啼时的：

My heart aches, and a drowsy numbness pains

My sense, as though of homlock I had drunk…

'Tis not through envy of thy happy lot,

But being too happy in thy happiness…

曼殊斐尔的声音之美，又是一个 Miracle。一个个音符从她脆弱的声带里颤动出来，都在我习于尘俗的耳中，启示着一种神奇的意境，仿佛蔚蓝的天空中一颗一颗的明星先后涌现。像听音乐似的，

[①] 原文为"开茨"（Keats），通译为"济慈"（1795~1821），英国诗人。——编者注

虽则明明你一生从不曾听过，但你总觉得好像曾经闻到过的，也许在梦里，也许在前生。她的声音，不仅引起你听觉的美感，而竟似直达你的心灵底里，抚摩你蕴而不宣的苦痛，温和你半冷半僵的希望，洗涤你窒碍性灵的俗累，增加你精神快乐的情调，仿佛凑住你灵魂的耳畔，私语你平日所冥想不得的仙界消息。我便此时回想，还不禁内动感激的悲慨，几于零泪；她是去了，她的音声笑貌也似蜃彩似的一翳不再，我只能学 Aft Vogler 之自慰，虔信：

Whose voice has gone forth,

But each survives for the melodist

When eternity affirms the conception of an hour.

……

Enough that he heard it once；

We shall hear it by and by.

曼殊斐尔，我前面说过，是肺痨病死的，我见她时正离她死不过半年。她那晚说话时，声音稍高，肺管中便如荻管似的呼呼作响，她每句语尾收顿时，总有些气促，颧颊间便也多添一层红润，我当时听出了她肺弱的音息，便觉得切心的难过，而同时她天才的兴奋，偏是逼迫她音度的提高，音愈高，肺嘶亦更呖呖，胸间的起伏，亦隐约可辨，可怜！我无奈何，只得将自己的声音特别地放低，希冀她也跟着放低些。果然很灵效，她也放低了不少，但不久她又似内感思想的戟刺，重复节节地高引。最后我再也不忍因我而多耗她珍贵的精力，并且也记得默里再三叮嘱 W 与 S 的话，就辞了出来，总计我进房至出房——她站在房口送我——不过二十分钟的时间。

我与她所讲的话也很有意味，但大部分是她对于英国当时最风行的几个小说家的批评——例如Rebecca West，Romer Wilson，Hutchingson，Swinnerton，等——恐怕因为一般人不稔悉，那类简约的评语不能引起相当的兴味所以从略。默里自己是现在英国中年的评论家中最有学有识的一人——他去年在牛津大学讲的"The problem of style"，有人誉为阿诺德①（Matthew Arnold）以后评论界最重要的一部贡献——而他总常常推尊曼殊斐尔，说她是评论的天才，有言必中肯的本能，所以我此刻要把她那晚随兴简评的珠沫，略过不讲，很觉得有些可惜。她说她方才从瑞士回来，在那里和罗素夫妇寓所相距颇近，常常说起东方的好处，所以她原来对中国景仰，更一进而为爱慕的热忱。她说她最爱读 Arthur Waley 所翻的中国诗，她说那样的艺术在西方真是一个 Wonderful Revelation。她说新近 Amy Lowell 译的很使她失望，她这里又用她爱用的短句"That's not the thing！"她问我译过没

---

① 原文为"安诺德"（Matthew Arnold），通译为"阿诺德"（1822~1888），英国文艺批评家。——编者注

有，她再三劝我应当试试，她以为中国诗只有中国人能译得好的。

她又问我是否也是写小说的，她又问中国顶喜欢契诃夫的哪几篇，译得怎么样，此外谁最有影响。

她问我最喜欢读哪几家小说，我说哈代、康拉德，她的眉梢耸了一耸，笑道：

"Isn't it! we have to go back to the old maters for good literature——the real thing! "

她问我回中国去打算怎么样，她希望我不进政治，她愤愤地说现代政治的世界，不论哪一国，只是一乱堆的残暴和罪恶。

后来说起她自己的著作。我说她的太是纯粹的艺术，恐怕一般人反而不认识，她说：

"That's just it, then of course, popularity is never the thing for us."

我说我以后也许有机会试翻她的小说，愿意先得作者本人的许可。她很高兴地说她当然愿意，就怕她的著作不值得翻译的劳力。

她盼望我早日回欧洲，将来如到瑞士再去找她，她说怎样地爱瑞士风景，日内瓦①湖怎样地妩媚，我那时就仿佛在湖心柔波间与她荡舟玩景。

Clear, placid Leman! …
Thy soft murmuring
Sounds sweet as if
A sister's voice reproved.
That I with stern delights should e'er
Have been so moved…Lord Byron

　　我当时就满口地答应，说将来回欧一定到瑞士去访她。

　　末了我恐怕她已经倦了，深恨与她相见之晚，但盼望将来还有再见的机会。她送我到房门口，与我很诚挚地握别。

　　将近一月前我得到消息说曼殊斐尔已经在法国的枫丹白露②去世。这一篇文字，我早已想写出来，但始终为笔懒，延到如今，岂知如今却变了成她的祭文了！

---

① 原文为"琴妮湖"，现通译为"日内瓦湖"，瑞士著名的风景区。——编者注
② 原文为"芳丹卜罗"，现通译为"枫丹白露"，法国著名的风景区。——编者注

BLISS:

THE SELECTED STORIES OF KATHERINE MANSFIELD

Katherine Mansfield

THE GARDEN PARTY

And after all the weather was ideal. They could not have had a more perfect day for a garden party if they had ordered it. Windless, warm, the sky without a cloud. Only the blue was veiled with a haze of light gold, as it is sometimes in early summer. The gardener had been up since dawn, mowing the lawns and sweeping them, until the grass and the dark flat rosettes where the daisy plants had been seemed to shine. As for the roses, you could not help feeling they understood that roses are the only flowers that impress people at garden parties; the only flowers that everybody is certain of knowing. Hundreds, yes, literally hundreds, had come out in a single night; the green bushes bowed down as though they had been visited by archangels.

Breakfast was not yet over before the men came to put up the marquee.

"Where do you want the marquee put, mother?"

"My dear child, it's no use asking me. I'm determined to leave everything to you children this year. Forget I am your mother. Treat me as an honoured guest."

But Meg could not possibly go and supervise the men. She had washed her hair before breakfast, and she sat drinking her coffee in a green turban, with a dark wet curl stamped on each cheek. Jose, the butterfly, always came down in a silk petticoat and a kimono jacket.

"You'll have to go, Laura, you're the artistic one."

Away Laura flew, still holding her piece of bread-and-butter. It's so delicious to have an excuse for eating out of doors, and besides, she loved having to arrange things; she always felt she could do it so much better than anybody else.

Four men in their shirt-sleeves stood grouped together on the garden path. They carried staves covered with rolls of canvas, and they had big tool-bags slung on their backs. They looked impressive. Laura wished now that she was not holding that piece of bread-and-butter, but there was nowhere to put it, and she couldn't possibly throw it away. She blushed and tried to look severe and even a little bit short-sighted as she came up to them.

"Good morning," she said, copying her mother's voice. But that sounded so fearfully affected that she was ashamed, and stammered like a little girl, "Oh—er—have you come-is it about the marquee?"

"That's right, miss," said the tallest of the men, a lanky,

freckled fellow, and he shifted his tool-bag, knocked back his straw hat and smiled down at her. "That's about it."

His smile was so easy, so friendly, that Laura recovered. What nice eyes he had, small, but such a dark blue? And now she looked at the others, they were smiling too. "Cheer up, we won't bite," their smile seemed to say. How very nice workmen were? And what a beautiful morning! She mustn't mention the morning, she must be business-like. The marquee.

"Well, what about the lily-lawn? Would that do?"

And she pointed to the lily-lawn with the hand that didn't hold the bread-and-butter. They turned, they stared in the direction. A little fat chap thrust out his under-lip, and the tall fellow frowned.

"I don't fancy it," said he. "Not conspicuous enough. You see, with a thing like a marquee," and he turned to Laura in his easy way, "you want to put it somewhere where it'll give you a bang slap in the eye, if you follow me."

Laura's upbringing made her wonder for a moment whether it was quite respectful of a workman to talk to her of bangs slap in the eye. But she did quite follow him.

"A corner of the tennis-court," she suggested. "But the band's going to be in one corner."

"H'm, going to have a band, are you?" said another of the

workmen. He was pale. He had a haggard look as his dark eyes scanned the tennis-court. What was he thinking?

"Only a very small band," said Laura gently. Perhaps he wouldn't mind so much if the band was quite small. But the tall fellow interrupted.

"Look here, miss, that's the place. Against those trees. Over there. That'll do fine."

Against the karakas. Then the karaka-trees would be hidden. And they were so lovely, with their broad, gleaming leaves, and their clusters of yellow fruit. They were like trees you imagined growing on a desert island, proud, solitary, lifting their leaves and fruits to the sun in a kind of silent splendour. Must they be hidden by a marquee?

They must. Already the men had shouldered their staves and were making for the place. Only the tall fellow was left. He bent down, pinched a sprig of lavender, put his thumb and forefinger to his nose and snuffed up the smell. When Laura saw the gesture she forgot all about the karakas in her wonder at him caring for things like that—caring for the smell of lavender. How many men that she knew would have done such a thing? Oh, how extraordinarily nice workmen were, she thought. Why couldn't she have workmen for friends rather than the silly boys she danced with and who came to

Sunday night supper? She would get on much better with men like these.

It's all the fault, she decided, as the tall fellow drew something on the back of an envelope, something that was to be looped up or left to hang, of these absurd class distinctions. Well, for her part, she didn't feel them. Not a bit, not an atom...And now there came the chock-chock of wooden hammers. Some one whistled, some one sang out, "Are you right there, Matey?" "Matey!" The friendliness of it, the—the—Just to prove how happy she was, just to show the tall fellow how at home she felt, and how she despised stupid conventions, Laura took a big bite of her bread-and-butter as she stared at the little drawing. She felt just like a work-girl.

"Laura, Laura, where are you? Telephone, Laura!" a voice cried from the house.

"Coming!" Away she skimmed, over the lawn, up the path, up the steps, across the veranda, and into the porch. In the hall her father and Laurie were brushing their hats ready to go to the office.

"I say, Laura," said Laurie very fast, "you might just give a squiz at my coat before this afternoon. See if it wants pressing."

"I will," said she. Suddenly she couldn't stop herself. She ran at Laurie and gave him a small, quick squeeze. "Oh, I do love parties, don't you?" gasped Laura.

"Rather," said Laurie's warm, boyish voice, and he squeezed his sister too, and gave her a gentle push. "Dash off to the telephone, old girl."

The telephone. "Yes, yes; oh yes. Kitty? Good morning, dear. Come to lunch? Do, dear. Delighted, of course. It will only be a very scratch meal—just the sandwich crusts and broken meringue-shells and what's left over. Yes, isn't a perfect morning? Your white? Oh, I certainly should. One moment—hold the line. Mother's calling." And Laura sat back. "What, mother? Can't hear."

Mrs Sheridan's voice floated down the stairs. "Tell her to wear that sweet hat she had on last Sunday."

"Mother says you're to wear that sweet hat you had on last Sunday. Good. One o'clock. Bye-bye."

Laura put back the receiver, flung her arms over her head, took a deep breath, stretched and let them fall. "Huh," she sighed, and the moment after the sigh she sat up quickly. She was still, listening. All the doors in the house seemed to be open. The house was alive with soft, quick steps and running voices. The green baize door that led to the kitchen regions swung open and shut with a muffled thud. And now there came a long, chuckling absurd sound. It was the heavy piano being moved on its stiff castors. But the air! If you stopped to notice, was the air always like this? Little faint winds were playing chase in at the tops of the windows, out at the doors. And there were two tiny spots of sun, one on the inkpot, one on a silver photograph frame, playing too. Darling little spots. Especially the one on the inkpot lid. It was quite warm. A warm little silver star. She could have kissed it.

The front door bell pealed, and there sounded the rustle of Sadie's print skirt on the stairs. A man's voice murmured; Sadie answered, careless, "I'm sure I don't know. Wait. I'll ask Mrs Sheridan."

"What is it, Sadie?" Laura came into the hall.

"It's the florist, Miss Laura."

It was, indeed. There, just inside the door, stood a wide, shallow tray full of pots of pink lilies. No other kind. Nothing but lilies—canna lilies, big pink flowers, wide open, radiant, almost frighteningly alive on bright crimson stems.

"O-oh, Sadie!" said Laura, and the sound was like a little moan. She crouched down as if to warm herself at that blaze of lilies; she felt they were in her fingers, on her lips, growing in her breast.

"It's some mistake," she said faintly. "Nobody ever ordered so many. Sadie, go and find mother."

But at that moment Mrs Sheridan joined them.

"It's quite right," she said calmly. "Yes, I ordered them. Aren't they lovely?" She pressed Laura's arm. "I was passing the shop yesterday, and I saw them in the window. And I suddenly thought for once in my life I shall have enough canna lilies. The garden party will be a good excuse."

"But I thought you said you didn't mean to interfere," said Laura. Sadie had gone. The florist's man was still outside at his van. She put her arm round her mother's neck and gently, very gently, she bit her mother's ear.

"My darling child, you wouldn't like a logical mother, would you? Don't do that. Here's the man."

He carried more lilies still, another whole tray.

"Bank them up, just inside the door, on both sides of the porch, please," said Mrs Sheridan. "Don't you agree, Laura?"

"Oh, I do, mother."

In the drawing-room, Meg, Jose and good little Hans had at last succeeded in moving the piano.

"Now, if we put this chesterfield against the wall and move everything out of the room except the chairs, don't you think?"

"Quite."

"Hans, move these tables into the smoking-room, and bring a sweeper to take these marks off the carpet and—one moment,

Hans—" Jose loved giving orders to the servants, and they loved obeying her. She always made them feel they were taking part in some drama. "Tell mother and Miss Laura to come here at once."

"Very good, Miss Jose."

She turned to Meg. "I want to hear what the piano sounds like, just in case I'm asked to sing this afternoon. Let's try over 'This life is Weary'."

Pom! Ta-ta-ta! Tee-ta! The piano burst out so passionately that Jose's face changed. She clasped her hands. She looked mournfully and enigmatically at her mother and Laura as they came in.

This Life is We—ary,
A Tear—A Sigh.
A Love that Chan—ges,
This Life is We—ary,
A Tear—A Sigh.
A Love that Chan—ges,
And then ... Good—bye!

But at the word "Good-bye", and although the piano sounded more desperate than ever, her face broke into a brilliant, dreadfully unsympathetic smile.

"Aren't I in good voice, mummy?" she beamed.

This Life is We-ary,
Hope comes to Die.
A Dream—A Wa-kening.

But now Sadie interrupted them. "What is it, Sadie?"

"If you please, m'm, cook says have you got the flags for the sandwiches?"

"The flags for the sandwiches, Sadie?" echoed Mrs Sheridan dreamily. And the children knew by her face that she hadn't got them. "Let me see." And she said to Sadie firmly, "Tell cook I'll let her have them in ten minutes."

Sadie went.

"Now, Laura," said her mother quickly, "come with me into the smoking-room. I've got the names somewhere on the back of an envelope. You'll have to write them out for me. Meg, go upstairs this minute and take that wet thing off your head. Jose, run and finish dressing this instant. Do you hear me, children, or shall I have to tell your father when he comes home tonight? And—and, Jose, pacify cook if you do go into the kitchen, will you? I'm terrified of her this morning."

The envelope was found at last behind the dining-room clock, though how it had got there Mrs Sheridan could not imagine.

"One of you children must have stolen it out of my bag, because I remember vividly—cream-cheese and lemon-curd. Have you done that?"

"Yes."

"Egg and—" Mrs Sheridan held the envelope away from her. "It looks like mice. It can't be mice, can it?"

"Olive, pet," said Laura, looking over her shoulder.

"Yes, of course, olive. What a horrible combination it sounds. Egg and olive."

They were finished at last, and Laura took them off to the kitchen. She found Jose there pacifying the cook, who did not look at all terrifying.

"I have never seen such exquisite sandwiches," said Jose's rapturous voice. "How many kinds did you say there were, cook? Fifteen?"

"Fifteen, Miss Jose."

"Well, cook, I congratulate you."

Cook swept up crusts with the long sandwich knife, and smiled broadly.

"Godber's has come," announced Sadie, issuing out of the pantry. She had seen the man pass the window.

That meant the cream puffs had come. Godber's were famous for their cream puffs. Nobody ever thought of making them at home.

"Bring them in and put them on the table, my girl," ordered

cook.

Sadie brought them in and went back to the door. Of course Laura and Jose were far too grown-up to really care about such things. All the same, they couldn't help agreeing that the puffs looked very attractive. Very. Cook began arranging them, shaking off the extra icing sugar.

"Don't they carry one back to all one's parties?" said Laura.

"I suppose they do," said practical Jose, who never liked to be carried back. "They look beautifully light and feathery, I must say."

"Have one each, my dears," said cook in her comfortable voice. "Your ma won't know."

Oh, impossible. Fancy cream puffs so soon after breakfast. The very idea made one shudder. All the same, two minutes later Jose and Laura were licking their fingers with that absorbed inward look that only comes from whipped cream.

"Let's go into the garden, out by the back way," suggested Laura. "I want to see how the men are getting on with the marquee. They're such awfully nice men."

But the back door was blocked by cook, Sadie, Godber's man and Hans.

Something had happened.

"Tuk-tuk-tuk," clucked cook like an agitated hen. Sadie had

her hand clapped to her cheek as though she had toothache. Hans's face was screwed up in the effort to understand. Only Godber's man seemed to be enjoying himself it was his story.

"What's the matter? What's happened?"

"There's been a horrible accident," said cook. "A man killed."

"A man killed! Where? How? When?"

But Godber's man wasn't going to have his story snatched from under his very nose.

"Know those little cottages just below here, miss?" Know them? Of course, she knew them. "Well, there's a young chap living there, name of Scott, a carter. His horse shied at a traction-engine, corner of Hawke Street this morning, and he was thrown out on the back of his head. Killed."

"Dead!" Laura stared at Godber's man.

"Dead when they picked him up," said Godber's man with relish. "They were taking the body home as I come up here." And he said to the cook, "He's left a wife and five little ones."

"Jose, come here." Laura caught hold of her sister's sleeve and dragged her through the kitchen to the other side of the green baize door. There she paused and leaned against it. "Jose!" she said, horrified, "however are we going to stop everything?"

"Stop everything, Laura!" cried Jose in astonishment. "What

do you mean?"

"Stop the garden party, of course." Why did Jose pretend?

But Jose was still more amazed. "Stop the garden party? My dear Laura, don't be so absurd. Of course we can't do anything of the kind. Nobody expects us to. Don't be so extravagant."

"But we can't possibly have a garden party with a man dead just outside the front gate."

That really was extravagant, for the little cottages were in a lane to themselves at the very bottom of a steep rise that led up to the house. A broad road ran between. True, they were far too near. They were the greatest possible eyesore, and they had no right to be in that neighbourhood at all. They were little mean dwellings painted a chocolate brown. In the garden patches there was nothing but cabbage stalks, sick hens and tomato cans. The very smoke coming out of their chimneys was poverty-stricken. Little rags and shreds of smoke, so unlike the great silvery plumes that uncurled from the Sheridans' chimneys. Washerwomen lived in the lane and sweeps and a cobbler, and a man whose house-front was studded all over with minute bird-cages. Children swarmed. When the Sheridans were little they were forbidden to set foot there because of the revolting language and of what they might catch. But since they were grown up, Laura and Laurie on their prowls sometimes walked through. It was disgusting and sordid. They came out with a shudder. But still one must go everywhere, one must see everything. So through they went.

"And just think of what the band would sound like to that poor woman," said Laura.

"Oh, Laura!" Jose began to be seriously annoyed. "If you're going to stop a band playing every time some one has an accident, you'll lead a very strenuous life. I'm every bit as sorry about it as you. I feel just as sympathetic." Her eyes hardened. She looked at her sister just as she used to when they were little and fighting together. "You won't bring a drunken workman back to life by being sentimental," she said softly.

"Drunk! Who said he was drunk?" Laura turned furiously on Jose. She said just as they had used to say on those occasions, "I'm going straight up to tell mother."

"Do, dear," cooed Jose.

"Mother, can I come into your room?" Laura turned the big glass door-knob.

"Of course, child. Why, what's the matter? What's given you such a colour?" And Mrs Sheridan turned round from her dressing-table. She was trying on a new hat.

"Mother, a man's been killed," began Laura.

"Not in the garden?" interrupted her mother.

"No, no!"

"Oh, what a fright you gave me!" Mrs Sheridan sighed with relief, and took off the big hat and held it on her knees.

"But listen, mother," said Laura. Breathless, half-choking, she told the dreadful story. "Of course, we can't have our party, can we?" she pleaded. "The band and everybody arriving. They'd hear us, mother; they're nearly neighbours!"

To Laura's astonishment her mother behaved just like Jose; it was harder to bear because she seemed amused. She refused to take Laura seriously.

"But, my dear child, use your common sense. It's only by accident we've heard of it. If some one had died there normally— and I can't understand how they keep alive in those poky little holes—we should still be having our party, shouldn't we?"

Laura had to say "yes" to that, but she felt it was all wrong. She sat down on her mother's sofa and pinched the cushion frill.

"Mother, isn't it really terribly heartless of us?" she asked.

"Darling!" Mrs Sheridan got up and came over to her, carrying the hat. Before Laura could stop her she had popped it on. "My child!" said her mother, "the hat is yours. It's made for you. It's much too young for me. I have never seen you look such a picture. Look at yourself!" And she held up her hand-mirror.

"But, mother," Laura began again. She couldn't look at herself, she turned aside.

This time Mrs Sheridan lost patience just as Jose had done.

"You are being very absurd, Laura," she said coldly. "People like that don't expect sacrifices from us. And it's not very sympathetic to spoil everybody's enjoyment as you're doing now."

"I don't understand," said Laura, and she walked quickly out of the room into her own bedroom. There, quite by chance, the first thing she saw was this charming girl in the mirror, in her black hat trimmed with gold daisies, and a long black velvet ribbon. Never had she imagined she could look like that. Is mother right? She thought. And now she hoped her mother was right. Am I being extravagant? Perhaps it was extravagant. Just for a moment she had another glimpse of that poor woman and those little children, and the body being carried into the house. But it all seemed blurred, unreal, like a picture in the newspaper. I'll remember it again after the party's over, she decided. And somehow that seemed quite the best plan…

Lunch was over by half-past one. By half-past two they were all ready for the fray. The green-coated band had arrived and was established in a corner of the tennis-court.

"My dear!" trilled Kitty Maitland, "aren't they too like frogs for words? You ought to have arranged them round the pond with the conductor in the middle on a leaf."

Laurie arrived and hailed them on his way to dress. At the sight of him Laura remembered the accident again. She wanted to tell him. If Laurie agreed with the others, then it was bound to be all right. And she followed him into the hall.

"Laurie!"

"Hallo?" He was half-way upstairs, but when he turned round and saw Laura he suddenly puffed out his cheeks and goggled his eyes at her. "My word, Laura! You do look stunning," said Laurie. "What an absolutely topping hat!"

Laura said faintly "Is it?" and smiled up at Laurie, and didn't tell him after all.

Soon after that people began coming in streams. The band struck up; the hired waiters ran from the house to the marquee. Wherever you looked there were couples strolling, bending to the flowers, greeting, moving on over the lawn. They were like bright birds that had alighted in the Sheridans' garden for this one afternoon, on their way to—where? Ah, what happiness it is to be with people who all are happy, to press hands, press cheeks, smile into eyes.

"Darling Laura, how well you look!"

"What a becoming hat, child!"

"Laura, you look quite Spanish. I've never seen you look so striking."

And Laura, glowing, answered softly, "Have you had tea? Won't you have an ice? The passion-fruit ices really are rather special." She ran to her father and begged him. "Daddy darling, can't the band have something to drink?"

And the perfect afternoon slowly ripened, slowly faded, slowly its petals closed.

"Never a more delightful garden party..." "The greatest success..." "Quite the most..."

Laura helped her mother with the good-byes. They stood side by side in the porch till it was all over.

"All over, all over, thank heaven," said Mrs Sheridan. "Round up the others, Laura. Let's go and have some fresh coffee. I'm exhausted. Yes, it's been very successful. But oh, these parties, these parties! Why will you children insist on giving parties?" And they all of them sat down in the deserted marquee.

"Have a sandwich, daddy dear. I wrote the flag."

"Thanks." Mr Sheridan took a bite and the sandwich was gone. He took another. "I suppose you didn't hear of a beastly accident that happened today?" he said.

"My dear," said Mrs Sheridan, holding up her hand, "we did.

It nearly ruined the party. Laura insisted we should put it off."

"Oh, mother!" Laura didn't want to be teased about it.

"It was a horrible affair all the same," said Mr Sheridan. "The chap was married too. Lived just below in the lane, and leaves a wife and half a dozen kiddies, so they say."

An awkward little silence fell. Mrs Sheridan fidgeted with her cup. Really, it was very tactless of father...

Suddenly she looked up. There on the table were all those sandwiches, cakes, puffs, all un-eaten, all going to be wasted. She had one of her brilliant ideas.

"I know," she said. "Let's make up a basket. Let's send that poor creature some of this perfectly good food. At any rate, it will be the greatest treat for the children. Don't you agree? And she's sure to have neighbours calling in and so on. What a point to have it all ready prepared. Laura!" She jumped up. "Get me the big basket out of the stairs cupboard."

"But, mother, do you really think it's a good idea?" said Laura.

Again, how curious, she seemed to be different from them all. To take scraps from their party. Would the poor woman really like that?

"Of course! What's the matter with you today? An hour or two ago you were insisting on us being sympathetic, and now—"

Oh well! Laura ran for the basket. It was filled, it was heaped by her mother.

"Take it yourself, darling," said she. "Run down just as you are. No, wait, take the arum lilies too. People of that class are so impressed by arum lilies."

"The stems will ruin her lace frock," said practical Jose.

So they would. Just in time. "Only the basket, then. And, Laura!"—her mother followed her out of the marquee—"don't on any account—"

"What mother?"

No, better not put such ideas into the child's head! "Nothing! Run along."

It was just growing dusky as Laura shut their garden gates. A big dog ran by like a shadow. The road gleamed white, and down below in the hollow the little cottages were in deep shade. How quiet it seemed after the afternoon. Here she was going down the hill to somewhere where a man lay dead, and she couldn't realize it. Why couldn't she? She stopped a minute. And it seemed to her that kisses, voices, tinkling spoons, laughter, the smell of crushed grass were somehow inside her. She had no room for anything else. How strange! She looked up at the pale sky, and all she thought was, "Yes, it was the most successful party."

Now the broad road was crossed. The lane began, smoky and dark. Women in shawls and men's tweed caps hurried by. Men hung over the palings; the children played in the doorways. A low hum came from the mean little cottages. In some of them there was a flicker of light, and a shadow, crab-like, moved across the window. Laura bent her head and hurried on. She wished now she had put on a coat. How her frock shone! And the big hat with the velvet streamer—if only it was another hat! Were the people looking at her? They must be. It was a mistake to have come; she knew all along it was a mistake. Should she go back even now?

No, too late. This was the house. It must be. A dark knot of people stood outside. Beside the gate an old, old woman with a crutch sat in a chair, watching. She had her feet on a newspaper. The voices stopped as Laura drew near. The group parted. It was as though she was expected, as though they had known she was coming here.

Laura was terribly nervous. Tossing the velvet ribbon over her shoulder, she said to a woman standing by, "Is this Mrs Scott's house?" and the woman, smiling queerly, said, "It is, my lass."

Oh, to be away from this! She actually said, "Help me, God," as she walked up the tiny path and knocked. To be away from those staring eyes, or to be covered up in anything, one of those women's shawls even. I'll just leave the basket and go, she decided. I shan't even wait for it to be emptied.

Then the door opened. A little woman in black showed in the gloom.

Laura said, "Are you Mrs Scott?" But to her horror the woman answered, "Walk in, please, miss," and she was shut in the passage.

"No," said Laura, "I don't want to come in. I only want to leave this basket. Mother sent—"

The little woman in the gloomy passage seemed not to have heard her. "Step this way, please, miss," she said in an oily voice, and Laura followed her.

She found herself in a wretched little low kitchen, lighted by a smoky lamp. There was a woman sitting before the fire.

"Em," said the little creature who had let her in. "Em! It's a young lady." She turned to Laura. She said meaningly, "I'm 'er sister, miss. You'll excuse 'er, won't you?"

"Oh, but of course!" said Laura. "Please, please don't disturb her. I—I only want to leave—"

But at that moment the woman at the fire turned round. Her face, puffed up, red, with swollen eyes and swollen lips, looked terrible. She seemed as though she couldn't understand why Laura was there. What did it mean? Why was this stranger standing in the kitchen with a basket? What was it all about? And the poor face puckered up again.

"All right, my dear," said the other. "I'll thank the young lady."

And again she began, "You'll excuse her, miss, I'm sure," and her face, swollen too, tried an oily smile.

Laura only wanted to get out, to get away. She was back in the passage. The door opened. She walked straight through into the bedroom where the dead man was lying.

"You'd like a look at 'im, wouldn't you?" said Em's sister, and she brushed past Laura over to the bed. "Don't be afraid, my lass," —and now her voice sounded fond and sly, and fondly she drew down the sheet— "'e looks a picture. There's nothing to show. Come along, my dear."

Laura came.

There lay a young man, fast asleep—sleeping so soundly, so deeply, that he was far, far away from them both. Oh, so remote, so peaceful. He was dreaming. Never wake him up again. His head was sunk in the pillow, his eyes were closed; they were blind under the closed eyelids. He was given up to his dream. What did garden parties and baskets and lace frocks matter to him? He was far from all those things. He was wonderful, beautiful. While they were laughing and while the band was playing, this marvel had come to the lane. Happy... happy... All is well, said that sleeping face. This is just as it should be. I am content.

But all the same you had to cry, and she couldn't go out of the room without saying something to him. Laura gave a loud childish sob.

"Forgive my hat," she said.

And this time she didn't wait for Em's sister. She found her way out of the door, down the path, past all those dark people. At the corner of the lane she met Laurie.

He stepped out of the shadow. "Is that you, Laura?"

"Yes."

"Mother was getting anxious. Was it all right?"

"Yes, quite. Oh, Laurie!" She took his arm, she pressed up against him.

"I say, you're not crying, are you?" asked her brother.

Laura shook her head. She was.

Laurie put his arm round her shoulder. "Don't cry," he said in his warm, loving voice. "Was it awful?"

"No," sobbed Laura. "It was simply marvellous. But, Laurie—" She stopped, she looked at her brother. "Isn't life," she stammered, "isn't life—" But what life was she couldn't explain. No matter. He quite understood.

"Isn't it, darling?" said Laurie.

POISON

The post was very late. When we came back from our walk after lunch it still had not arrived.

"*Pas encore*, Madame," sang Annette, scurrying back to her cooking.

We carried our parcels into the dining-room. The table was laid. As always, the sight of the table laid for two—for two people only—and yet so finished, so perfect, there was no possible room for a third, gave me a queer, quick thrill as though I'd been struck by that silver lightning that quivered over the white cloth, the brilliant glasses, the shadow bowl of freesias.

"Blow the old postman! Whatever can have happened to him?" said Beatrice. "Put those things down, dearest."

"Where would you like them...?"

She raised her head; she smiled her sweet, teasing smile.

"Anywhere—Silly."

But I knew only too well that there was no such place for her, and I would have stood holding the squat liqueur bottle and the sweets for months, for years, rather than risk giving another tiny shock to her exquisite sense of order.

"Here—I'll take them." She plumped them down on the table with her long gloves and a basket of figs. "The Luncheon Table. Short story by—by—" She took my arm. "Let's go on to the terrace—" and I felt her shiver. "Ça sent," she said faintly, "*de la cuisine...*"

I had noticed lately—we had been living in the south for two months—that when she wished to speak of food, or the climate, or, playfully, of her love for me, she always dropped into French.

We perched on the balustrade under the awning. Beatrice leaned over gazing down—down to the white road with its guard of cactus spears. The beauty of her ear, just her ear, the marvel of it was so great that I could have turned from regarding it to all that sweep of glittering sea below and stammered: "You know—her ear! She has ears that are simply the most..."

She was dressed in white, with pearls round her throat and lilies-of-the-valley tucked into her belt. On the third finger of her left hand she wore one pearl ring—no wedding-ring.

"Why should I, *mon ami*? Why should we pretend? Who could possibly care?"

And of course I agreed, though privately, in the depths of my heart, I would have given my soul to have stood beside her in a large, yes, a large, fashionable church, crammed with people, with old reverend clergymen, with *The Voice that breathed o'er Eden*, with palms and the smell of scent, knowing there was a red carpet and confetti outside, and somewhere, a wedding-cake and champagne and a satin shoe to throw after the carriage—if I could have slipped our wedding-ring on to her finger.

Not because I cared for such horrible shows, but because I felt it might possibly perhaps lessen this ghastly feeling of absolute freedom, her absolute freedom, of course.

Oh, God! What torture happiness was—what anguish! I looked up at the villa, at the windows of our room hidden so mysteriously behind the green straw blinds. Was it possible that she ever came moving through the green light and smiling that secret smile, that languid, brilliant smile that was just for me? She put her arm round my neck; the other hand softly, terribly, brushed back my hair.

"Who are you?" Who was she? She was—Woman.

... On the first warm evening in spring, when lights shone like pearls through the lilac air and voices murmured in the fresh-flowering gardens, it was she who sang in the tall house with the tulle curtains. As one drove in the moonlight through the foreign city hers was the shadow that fell across the quivering gold of the shutters. When the lamp was lighted, in the newborn stillness her steps passed your door. And she looked out into the autumn twilight, pale in her furs, as the automobile swept by...

In fact, to put it shortly, I was twenty-four at the time. And when she lay on her back, with the pearls slipped under her chin, and sighed "I'm thirsty, dearest. *Donne–moi un orange*," I would gladly, willingly, have dived for an orange into the jaws of a crocodile—if crocodiles ate oranges.

> *"Had I two little feathery wings*
> *And were a little feathery bird..."*

sang Beatrice.

I seized her hand. "You wouldn't fly away?"

"Not far. Not further than the bottom of the road."

"Why on earth there?"

She quoted: "He cometh not, she said..."

"Who? The silly old postman? But you're not expecting a letter."

"No, but it's maddening all the same. Ah!" Suddenly she laughed and leaned against me. "There he is—look—like a blue beetle."

And we pressed our cheeks together and watched the blue beetle beginning to climb.

"Dearest," breathed Beatrice. And the word seemed to linger

in the air, to throb in the air like the note of a violin.

"What is it?"

"I don't know," she laughed softly. "A wave of—a wave of affection, I suppose."

I put my arm round her. "Then you wouldn't fly away?"

And she said rapidly and softly: "No? No? Not for worlds. Not really. I love this place. I've loved being here. I could stay here for years, I believe. I've never been so happy as I have these last two months, and you've been so perfect to me, dearest, in every way."

This was such bliss—it was so extraordinary, so unprecedented, to hear her talk like this that I had to try to laugh it off.

"Don't! You sound as if you were saying good-bye."

"Oh, nonsense, nonsense. You mustn't say such things even in fun!" She slid her little hand under my white jacket and clutched my shoulder. "You've been happy, haven't you?"

"Happy? Happy? Oh, God—if you knew what I feel at this moment...Happy! My Wonder! My Joy!"

I dropped off the balustrade and embraced her, lifting her in my arms. And while I held her lifted I pressed my face in her breast and muttered: "You are mine?" And for the first time in all the desperate months I'd known her, even counting the last month of—

surely—Heaven—I believed her absolutely when she answered:

"Yes, I am yours."

The creek of the gate and the postman's steps on the gravel drew us apart. I was dizzy for the moment. I simply stood there, smiling, I felt, rather stupidly. Beatrice walked over to the cane chairs.

"You go—go for the letters," said she.

I—well—I almost reeled away. But I was too late. Annette came running. "*Pas de lettres*," said she.

My reckless smile in reply as she handed me the paper must have surprised her. I was wild with joy. I threw the paper up into the air and sang out:

"No letters, darling!" as I came over to where the beloved woman was lying in the long chair.

For a moment she did not reply. Then she said slowly as she tore off the newspaper wrapper: "The world forgetting, by the world forgot."

There are times when a cigarette is just the very one thing that will carry you over the moment. It is more than a confederate, even; it is a secret, perfect, little friend who knows all about it and understands absolutely. While you smoke you look down at it— smile or frown, as the occasion demands; you inhale deeply and expel the smoke in a slow fan. This was one of those moments. I walked over to the magnolia and breathed my fill of it. Then I came back and leaned over her shoulder. But quickly she tossed the paper away on to the stone.

"There's nothing in it," said she. "Nothing. There's only some poison trial. Either some man did or didn't murder his wife, and twenty thousand people have sat in court every day and two million words have been wired all over the world after each proceeding."

"Silly world!" said I, flinging into another chair. I wanted to forget the paper, to return, but cautiously, of course, to that moment before the postman came. But when she answered I knew from her voice the moment was over for now. Never mind. I was content to wait—five hundred years, if need be— now that I knew.

"Not so very silly," said Beatrice. "After all, it isn't only morbid curiosity on the part of the twenty thousand."

"What is it, darling?" Heaven knows I didn't care.

"Guilt!" she cried. "Guilt! Didn't you realize that? They're fascinated like sick people are fascinated by anything— any scrap of news about their own case. The man in the dock may be innocent enough, but the people in court are nearly all of them poisoners. Haven't you ever thought"—she was pale with excitement—"of the amount of poisoning that goes on? It's the exception to find married people who don't poison each other—married people and lovers. Oh," she cried, "the number of cups of tea, glasses of wine, cups of coffee that are just tainted. The number I've had myself, and drunk, either knowing or not knowing—and risked it. The only reason why so many couples" —she laughed—"survive, is because the one is frightened of giving the other the fatal dose. That dose takes nerve! But it's bound to come sooner or later. There's no going back once the first little dose has been given. It's the beginning of the end, really—don't you agree? Don't you see what I mean?"

She didn't wait for me to answer. She unpinned the lilies-of-the-valley and lay back, drawing them across her eyes.

"Both my husbands poisoned me," said Beatrice. "My first husband gave me a huge dose almost immediately, but my second was really an artist in his way. Just a tiny pinch, now and again, cleverly disguised—Oh, so cleverly!—until one morning I woke up and in every single particle of me, to the ends of my fingers and toes, there was a tiny grain. I was just in time..."

I hated to hear her mention her husbands so calmly, especially today. It hurt. I was going to speak, but suddenly she cried mournfully:

"Why! Why should it have happened to me? What have I done? Why have I been all my life singled out by...It's a conspiracy."

I tried to tell her it was because she was too perfect for this horrible world—too exquisite, too fine. It frightened people. I made a little joke.

"But I—I haven't tried to poison you."

Beatrice gave a queer small laugh and bit the end of a lily stem.

"You!" said she. "You wouldn't hurt a fly!"

Strange. That hurt, though. Most horribly.

Just then Annette ran out with our apéritifs. Beatrice leaned forward and took a glass from the tray and handed it to me. I noticed the gleam of the pearl on what I called her pearl finger. How could I be hurt at what she said?

"And you," I said, taking the glass, "you've never poisoned anybody."

That gave me an idea; I tried to explain. "You—you do just the opposite. What is the name for one like you who, instead of poisoning people, fills them—everybody, the postman, the man who drives us, our boatman, the flower-seller, me—with new life, with something of her own radiance, her beauty, her—"

Dreamily she smiled; dreamily she looked at me.

"What are you thinking of—my lovely darling?"

"I was wondering," she said, "whether, after lunch, you'd go down to the post-office and ask for the afternoon letters. Would you mind, dearest? Not that I'm expecting one —but—I just thought, perhaps—it's silly not to have the letters if they're there. Isn't it? Silly to wait till tomorrow." She twirled the stem of the glass in her fingers. Her beautiful head was bent. But I lifted my glass and drank, sipped rather—sipped slowly, deliberately, looking at that dark head and thinking of—postmen and blue beetles and farewells that were not farewells and...

Good God! Was it fancy? No, it wasn't fancy. The drink tasted chill, bitter, queer.

LIFE OF MA PARKER

When the literary gentleman, whose flat old Ma Parker cleaned every Tuesday, opened the door to her that morning, he asked after her grandson. Ma Parker stood on the doormat inside the dark little hall, and she stretched out her hand to help her gentleman shut the door before she replied. "We buried 'im yesterday, sir," she said quietly.

"Oh, dear me! I'm sorry to hear that," said the literary gentleman in a shocked tone. He was in the middle of his breakfast. He wore a very shabby dressing-gown and carried a crumpled newspaper in one hand. But he felt awkward. He could hardly go back to the warm sitting-room without saying something— something more. Then because these people set such store by funerals he said kindly, "I hope the funeral went off all right."

"Beg padding, sir?" said old Ma Parker huskily.

Poor old bird! She did look dashed. "I hope the funeral was a—a—success," said he. Ma Parker gave no answer. She bent her head and hobbled off to the kitchen, clasping the old fish bag that held her cleaning things and an apron and a pair of felt shoes.

The literary gentleman raised his eyebrows and went back to his breakfast.

"Overcome, I suppose," he said aloud, helping himself to the marmalade.

Ma Parker drew the two jetty spears out of her toque and hung it behind the door. She unhooked her worn jacket and hung that up too. Then she tied her apron and sat down to take off her boots. To take off her boots or to put them on was an agony to her, but it had been an agony for years. In fact, she was so accustomed to the pain that her face was drawn and screwed up ready for the twinge before she'd so much as untied the laces. That over, she sat back with a sigh and softly rubbed her knees...

"Gran! Gran!" Her little grandson stood on her lap in his button boots. He'd just come in from playing in the street.

"Look what a state you've made your gran's skirt into—you wicked boy?"

But he put his arms round her neck and rubbed his cheek against hers.

"Gran, gi' us a penny!" he coaxed.

"Be off with you; Gran ain't got no pennies."

"Yes, you 'ave."

"No, I ain't."

"Yes, you 'ave. Gi' us one!"

Already she was feeling for the old, squashed, black leather purse.

"Well, what'll you give your gran?"

He gave a shy little laugh and pressed closer. She felt his eyelid quivering against her cheek. "I ain't got anything," he murmured...

The old woman sprang up, seized the iron kettle off the gas stove and took it over to the sink. The noise of the water drumming in the kettle deadened her pain, it seemed. She filled the pail, too, and the washing-up bowl.

It would take a whole book to describe the state of that kitchen. During the week the literary gentleman "did" for himself. That is to say, he emptied the tea-leaves now and again into a jam jar set aside for that purpose, and if he ran out of clean forks he wiped over one or two on the roller towel. Otherwise, as he explained to his friends, his "system" was quite simple, and he couldn't understand why people made all this fuss about housekeeping.

"You simply dirty everything you've got, get a hag in once a week to clean up, and the things done."

The result looked like a gigantic dustbin. Even the floor was littered with toast crusts, envelopes, cigarette ends. But Ma Parker bore him no grudge. She pitied the poor young gentleman for having no one to look after him. Out of the smudgy little window you could see an immense expanse of sad-looking sky, and whenever there were clouds they looked very worn, old clouds, frayed at the edges, with holes in them, or dark stains like tea.

While the water was heating, Ma Parker began sweeping the floor. "Yes," she thought, as the broom knocked, "what with one thing and another I've had my share. I've had a hard life."

Even the neighbors said that of her. Many a time, hobbling home with her fish bag, she heard them, waiting at the corner, or leaning over the area railings, say among themselves, "She's had a hard life, has Ma Parker." And it was so true she wasn't in the least proud of it. It was just as if you were to say she lived in the basement-back at Number 27. A hard life! ...

At sixteen she'd left Stratford and come up to London as kitchen-maid. Yes, she was born in Stratford-on-Avon. Shakespeare, sir? No, people were always asking her about him. But she'd never heard his name until she saw it on the theatres.

Nothing remained of Stratford except that "sitting in the fireplace of a evening you could see the stars through the chimney", and "Mother always 'ad 'er side of bacon 'anging from the ceiling". And there was something—a bush, there was—at the front door, that smelt ever so nice. But the bush was very vague. She'd only remembered it once or twice in the hospital, when she'd been taken bad.

That was a dreadful place—her first place. She was never allowed out. She never went upstairs except for prayers morning and evening. It was a fair cellar. And the cook was a cruel woman. She used to snatch away her letters from home before she 'd read them, and throw them in the range because they made her dreamy...And the beetles! Would you believe it? —Until she came to London she'd never seen a black beetle. Here Ma always gave a little laugh, as though—not to have seen a black beetle! Well! It was as if to say you'd never seen your own feet.

When that family was sold up she went as "help" to a doctor's house, and after two years there, on the run from morning till night, she married her husband. He was a baker.

"A baker, Mrs Parker!" the literary gentleman would say. For occasionally he laid aside his times and lent an ear, at least, to this product called Life. "It must be rather nice to be married to a baker?"

Mrs Parker didn't look so sure.

"Such a clean trade," said the gentleman.

Mrs Parker didn't look convinced.

"And didn't you like handing the new loaves to the customers?"

"Well, sir," said Mrs Parker, "I wasn't in the shop above a great deal. We had thirteen little ones and buried seven of them. If it wasn't the 'ospital it was the infirmary, you might say?"

"You might, indeed, Mrs Parker!" said the gentleman, shuddering, and taking up his pen again.

Yes, seven had gone, and while the six were still small her husband was taken ill with consumption. It was flour on the lungs, the doctor told her at the time...Her husband sat up in bed with his shirt pulled over his head, and the doctor's finger drew a circle on his back.

"Now, if we were to cut him open here, Mrs Parker," said the doctor, "you'd find his lungs chock-a-block with white powder. Breathe, my good fellow!" And Mrs Parker never knew for certain whether she saw or whether she fancied she saw a great fan of white dust come out of her poor dear husband's lips...

But the struggle she'd had to bring up those six little children and keep herself to herself. Terrible it had been! Then, just when they were old enough to go to school her husband's sister came to stop with them to help things along, and she hadn't been there more than two months when she fell down a flight of steps and hurt her spine. And for five years Ma Parker had another baby—and such a one for crying—to look after. Then young Maudie went wrong and took her sister Alice with her; the two boys emigrated, and young Jim went to India with the army, and Ethel, the youngest, married a good-for-nothing little waiter who died of ulcers the year little Lennie was born. And now little Lennie—my grandson...

The piles of dirty cups, dirty dishes, were washed and dried. The ink-black knives were cleaned with a piece of potato and finished off with a piece of cork. The table was scrubbed, and the dresser and the sink that had sardine tails swimming in it...

He'd never been a strong child—never from the first. He'd been one of those fair babies that everybody took for a girl. Silvery fair curls he had, blue eyes, and a little freckle like a diamond on one side of his nose. The trouble she and Ethel had had to rear that child! The things out of the newspapers they tried him with! Every Sunday morning Ethel would read aloud while Ma Parker did her washing.

"DEAR SIR,—Just a line to let you know my little Myrtil was laid out for dead... After four bottles... gained 8 lbs. in 9 weeks, and is still putting it on."

And then the egg-cup of ink would come off the dresser and the letter would be written, and Ma would buy a postal order on her way to work next morning. But it was no use. Nothing made little Lennie put it on. Taking him to the cemetery, even, never gave him a colour; a nice shake-up in the bus never improved his appetite.

But he was gran's boy from the first...

"Whose boy are you?" said old Ma Parker, straightening up from the stove and going over to the smudgy window. And a little voice, so warm, so close, it half stifled her—it seemed to be in her breast under her heart—laughed out, and said, "I'm gran's boy!"

At that moment there was a sound of steps, and the literary gentleman appeared, dressed for walking.

"Oh, Mrs Parker, I'm going out."

"Very good, sir."

"And you'll find your half-crown in the tray of the inkstand."

"Thank you, sir."

"Oh, by the way, Mrs Parker," said the literary gentleman quickly, "you didn't throw away any cocoa last time you were here—did you?"

"No, sir."

"Very strange. I could have sworn I left a teaspoonful of cocoa in the tin." He broke off. He said softly and firmly, "You'll always tell me when you throw things away—won't you, Mrs Parker?" And he walked off very well pleased with himself, convinced, in fact, he'd shown Mrs Parker that under his apparent carelessness he was as vigilant as a woman.

The door banged. She took her brushes and cloths into the bedroom. But when she began to make the bed, smoothing, tucking, patting, the thought of little Lennie was unbearable. Why did he have to suffer so? That's what she couldn't understand. Why should a little angel child have to ask for his breath and fight for it? There was no sense in making a child suffer like that.

... From Lennie's little box of a chest there came a sound as though something was boiling. There was a great lump of something bubbling in his chest that he couldn't get rid of. When he coughed, the sweat sprang out on his head; his eyes bulged, his hands waved, and the great lump bubbled as a potato knocks in a saucepan. But what was more awful than all was when he didn't cough he sat against the pillow and never spoke or answered, or even made as if he heard. Only he looked offended.

"It's not your poor old gran's doing it, my lovey," said old Ma Parker, patting back the damp hair from his scarlet ears. But Lennie moved his head and edged away. Dreadfully offended with her he looked—and solemn. He bent his head and looked at her sideways as though he couldn't have believed it of his gran.

But at the last...Ma Parker threw the counterpane over the bed.

No, she simply couldn't think about it. It was too much —she'd had too much in her life to bear. She'd borne it up till now, she'd kept herself to herself, and never once had she been seen to cry. Never by a living soul. Not even her own children had seen Ma break down. She'd kept a proud face always. But now! Lennie gone—what had she? She had nothing. He was all she'd got from life, and now he was took too. Why must it all have happened to me? She wondered. "What have I done?" said old Ma Parker. "What have I done?"

As she said those words she suddenly let fall her brush. She found herself in the kitchen. Her misery was so terrible that she pinned on her hat, put on her jacket and walked out of the flat like a person in a dream. She did not know what she was doing. She was like a person so dazed by the horror of what has happened that he walks away— anywhere, as though by walking away he could escape...

It was cold in the street. There was a wind like ice. People went flitting by, very fast; the men walked like scissors; the women trod like cats. And nobody knew—nobody cared. Even if she broke down, if at last, after all these years, she were to cry, she'd find herself in the lock-up as like as not.

But at the thought of crying it was as though little Lennie leapt in his gran's arms. Ah, that's what she wants to do, my dove. Gran wants to cry. If she could only cry now, cry for a long time, over everything, beginning with her first place and the cruel cook, going on to the doctor's, and then the seven little ones, death of her husband, the children's leaving her, and all the years of misery that led up to Lennie. But to have a proper cry over all these things would take a long time. All the same, the time for it had come. She must do it. She couldn't put it off any longer; she couldn't wait any more...Where could she go?

"She's had a hard life, has Ma Parker." Yes, a hard life, indeed! Her chin began to tremble; there was no time to lose. But where? Where?

She couldn't go home; Ethel was there. It would frighten Ethel out of her life. She couldn't sit on a bench anywhere; people would come asking her questions. She couldn't possibly go back to the gentleman's flat; she had no right to cry in strangers' houses. If she sat on some steps, a policeman would speak to her.

Oh, wasn't there anywhere where she could hide and keep herself to herself and stay as long as she liked, not disturbing anybody, and nobody worrying her? Wasn't there anywhere in the world where she could have her cry out—at last?

Ma Parker stood, looking up and down. The icy wind blew out her apron into a balloon. And now it began to rain. There was nowhere.

A CUP OF TEA

Rosemary Fell was not exactly beautiful. No, you couldn't have called her beautiful. Pretty? Well, if you took her to pieces... But why be so cruel as to take anyone to pieces? She was young, brilliant, extremely modern, exquisitely well dressed, amazingly well read in the newest of the new books, and her parties were the most delicious mixture of the really important people and... artists—quaint creatures, discoveries of hers, some of them too terrifying for words, but others quite presentable and amusing.

Rosemary had been married two years. She had a duck of a boy. No, not Peter—Michael. And her husband absolutely adored her. They were rich, really rich, not just comfortably well off, which is odious and stuffy and sounds like one's grandparents. But if Rosemary wanted to shop she would go to Paris as you and I would go to Bond Street. If she wanted to buy flowers, the car pulled up at that perfect shop in Regent Street, and Rosemary inside the shop just gazed in her dazzled, rather exotic way, and said: "I want those and those and those. Give me four bunches of those. And that jar of roses. Yes, I'll have all the roses in the jar.

No, no lilac. I hate lilac. It's got no shape." The attendant bowed and put the lilac out of sight, as though this was only too true; lilac was dreadfully shapeless. "Give me those stumpy little tulips. Those red and white ones." And she was followed to the car by a thin shop-girl staggering under an immense white paper armful that looked like a baby in long clothes...

One winter afternoon she had been buying something in a little antique shop in Curzon Street. It was a shop she liked. For one thing, one usually had it to oneself. And then the man who kept it was ridiculously fond of serving her. He beamed whenever she came in. He clasped his hands; he was so gratified he could scarcely speak. Flattery, of course. All the same, there was something...

"You see, madam," he would explain in his low respectful tones, "I love my things. I would rather not part with them than sell them to someone who does not appreciate them, who has not that fine feeling which is so rare..." And, breathing deeply, he unrolled a tiny square of blue velvet and pressed it on the glass counter with his pale finger-tips.

Today it was a little box. He had been keeping it for her. He had shown it to nobody as yet. An exquisite little enamel box with a glaze so fine it looked as though it had been baked in cream. On the lid a minute creature stood under a flowery tree, and a more minute creature still had her arms round his neck. Her hat, really no bigger than a geranium petal, hung from a branch; it had green ribbons. And there was a pink cloud like a watchful cherub floating above their heads. Rosemary took her hands out of her long gloves. She always took off her gloves to examine such things. Yes, she liked it very much. She loved it; it was a great duck. She must have it. And, turning the creamy box, opening and shutting it, she couldn't help noticing how charming her hands were against the blue velvet. The shopman, in some dim cavern of his mind, may have dared to think so too. For he took a pencil, leant over the counter, and his pale bloodless fingers crept timidly towards those rosy, flashing ones, as he murmured gently: "If I may venture to point out to madam, the flowers on the little lady's bodice."

"Charming!" Rosemary admired the flowers. But what was the price? For a moment the shopman did not seem to hear. Then a murmur reached her. "Twenty-eight guineas, madam."

"Twenty-eight guineas." Rosemary gave no sign. She laid the little box down; she buttoned her gloves again. Twenty-eight guineas. Even if one is rich...She looked vague. She stared at a plump tea-kettle like a plump hen above the shopman's head, and her voice was dreamy as she answered: "Well, keep it for me—will you? I'll..."

But the shopman had already bowed as though keeping it for her was all any human being could ask. He would be willing, of course, to keep it for her forever.

The discreet door shut with a click. She was outside on the step, gazing at the winter afternoon. Rain was falling, and with the rain it seemed the dark came too, spinning down like ashes. There was a cold bitter taste in the air, and the new-lighted lamps looked sad. Sad were the lights in the houses opposite. Dimly they burned as if regretting something. And people hurried by, hidden under their hateful umbrellas. Rosemary felt a strange pang. She pressed her muff against her breast; she wished she had the little box, too, to cling to. Of course, the car was there. She'd only to cross the pavement. But still she waited. There are moments, horrible moments in life, when one emerges from shelter and looks out, and it's awful. One oughtn't to give way to them. One ought to go home and have an extra-special tea. But at the very instant of thinking that, a young girl, thin, dark, shadowy—where had she come from?—was standing at Rosemary's elbow and a voice like a sigh, almost like a sob, breathed: "Madam, may I speak to you a moment?"

"Speak to me?" Rosemary turned. She saw a little battered creature with enormous eyes, someone quite young, no older than herself, who clutched at her coat-collar with reddened hands, and shivered as though she had just come out of the water.

"M-madam," stammered the voice. "Would you let me have

the price of a cup of tea?"

"A cup of tea?" There was something simple, sincere in that voice; it wasn't in the least the voice of a beggar. "Then have you no money at all?" asked Rosemary.

"None, madam," came the answer.

"How extraordinary!" Rosemary peered through the dusk, and the girl gazed back at her. How more than extraordinary! And suddenly it seemed to Rosemary such an adventure. It was like something out of a novel by Dostoevsky, this meeting in the dusk. Supposing she took the girl home? Supposing she did do one of those things she was always reading about or seeing on the stage, what would happen? It would be thrilling. And she heard herself saying afterwards to the amazement of her friends: "I simply took her home with me," as she stepped forward and said to that dim person beside her: "Come home to tea with me."

The girl drew back startled. She even stopped shivering for a moment. Rosemary put out a hand and touched her arm. "I mean it," she said, smiling. And she felt how simple and kind her smile was. "Why won't you? Do. Come home with me now in my car and have tea."

"You—you don't mean it, madam," said the girl, and there was pain in her voice.

"But I do," cried Rosemary. "I want you to. To please me.

Come along."

The girl put her fingers to her lips and her eyes devoured Rosemary. "You're—you're not taking me to the police station?" she stammered.

"The police station!" Rosemary laughed out. "Why should I be so cruel? No, I only want to make you warm and to hear—anything you care to tell me."

Hungry people are easily led. The footman held the door of the car open, and a moment later they were skimming through the dusk.

"There!" said Rosemary. She had a feeling of triumph as she slipped her hand through the velvet strap. She could have said, "Now I've got you," as she gazed at the little captive she had netted. But of course she meant it kindly. Oh, more than kindly. She was going to prove to this girl that—wonderful things did happen in life, that—fairy godmothers were real, that—rich people had hearts, and that women were sisters. She turned impulsively, saying: "Don't be frightened. After all, why shouldn't you come back with me? We're both women. If I'm the more fortunate, you ought to expect..."

But happily at that moment, for she didn't know how the sentence was going to end, the car stopped. The bell was rung, the door opened, and with a charming, protecting, almost embracing movement, Rosemary drew the other into the hall. Warmth, softness, light, a sweet scent, all those things so familiar to her she never even thought about them, she watched that other receive. It was fascinating. She was like the rich little girl in her nursery with all the cupboards to open, all the boxes to unpack.

"Come, come upstairs," said Rosemary, longing to begin to be generous. "Come up to my room." And, besides, she wanted to spare this poor little thing from being stared at by the servants; she decided as they mounted the stairs she would not even ring for Jeanne, but take off her things by herself. The great thing was to be natural!

And, "There?" cried Rosemary again, as they reached her beautiful big bedroom with the curtains drawn, the fire leaping on her wonderful lacquer furniture, her gold cushions and the primrose and blue rugs.

The girl stood just inside the door; she seemed dazed. But Rosemary didn't mind that.

"Come and sit down," she cried, dragging her big chair up to the fire, "in this comfy chair. Come and get warm. You look so dreadfully cold."

"I daren't, madam," said the girl, and she edged backwards.

"Oh, please,"—Rosemary ran forward—"you mustn't be frightened, you mustn't, really. Sit down, and when I've taken off my things we shall go into the next room and have tea and be cosy.

Why are you afraid?" And gently she half pushed the thin figure into its deep cradle.

But there was no answer. The girl stayed just as she had been put, with her hands by her sides and her mouth slightly open. To be quite sincere, she looked rather stupid. But Rosemary wouldn't acknowledge it. She leant over her, saying: "Won't you take off your hat? Your pretty hair is all wet. And one is so much more comfortable without a hat, isn't one?"

There was a whisper that sounded like "very good, madam", and the crushed hat was taken off.

"And let me help you off with your coat, too," said Rosemary.

The girl stood up. But she held on to the chair with one hand and let Rosemary pull. It was quite an effort. The other scarcely helped her at all. She seemed to stagger like a child, and the thought came and went through Rosemary's mind, that if people wanted helping they must respond a little, just a little, otherwise it became very difficult indeed. And what was she to do with the coat now? She left it on the floor and the hat too. She was just going to take a cigarette off the mantelpiece when the girl said quickly, but so lightly and strangely: "I'm very sorry, madam, but I'm going to faint. I shall go off, madam, if I don't have something."

"Good heavens, how thoughtless I am!" Rosemary rushed to

the bell.

"Tea! Tea at once! And some brandy immediately!"

The maid was gone again, but the girl almost cried out: "No, I don't want no brandy. I never drink brandy. It's a cup of tea I want, madam." And she burst into tears.

It was a terrible and fascinating moment. Rosemary knelt beside her chair.

"Don't cry, poor little thing," she said. "Don't cry." And she gave the other her lace handkerchief. She really was touched beyond words. She put her arm round those thin, bird-like shoulders.

Now at last the other forgot to be shy, forgot everything except that they were both women, and gasped out: "I can't go on no longer like this. I can't bear it. I can't bear it. I shall do away with myself. I can't bear no more."

"You shan't have to. I'll look after you. Don't cry any more. Don't you see what a good thing it was that you met me? We'll have tea and you'll tell me everything. And I shall arrange something. I promise. Do stop crying. It's so exhausting. Please?"

The other did stop just in time for Rosemary to get up before the tea came. She had the table placed between them. She plied the poor little creature with everything, all the sandwiches, all the bread and butter, and every time her cup was empty she filled it with tea, cream and sugar. People always said sugar was so nourishing. As for herself she didn't eat; she smoked and looked away tactfully so that the other should not be shy.

And really the effect of that slight meal was marvellous. When the tea-table was carried away a new being, a light, frail creature with tangled hair, dark lips, deep, lighted eyes, lay back in the big chair in a kind of sweet languor, looking at the blaze. Rosemary lit a fresh cigarette; it was time to begin.

"And when did you have your last meal?" she asked softly.

But at that moment the door-handle turned.

"Rosemary, may I come in?" It was Philip.

"Of course."

He came in. "Oh, I'm so sorry," he said, and stopped and stared.

"It's quite all right," said Rosemary, smiling. "This is my friend, Miss—"

"Smith, madam," said the languid figure, who was strangely still and unafraid.

"Smith," said Rosemary. "We are going to have a little talk."

"Oh yes," said Philip. "Quite," and his eye caught sight of the coat and hat on the floor. He came over to the fire and turned his back to it. "It's a beastly afternoon," he said curiously, still looking at that listless figure, looking at her hands and boots, and then at Rosemary again.

"Yes, isn't it?" said Rosemary enthusiastically. "Vile."

Philip smiled his charming smile. "As a matter of fact," said he, "I wanted you to come into the library for a moment. Would you? Will Miss Smith excuse us?"

The big eyes were raised to him, but Rosemary answered for her: "Of course she will." And they went out of the room together.

"I say," said Philip, when they were alone. "Explain. Who is she? What does it all mean?"

Rosemary, laughing, leaned against the door and said: "I picked her up in Curzon Street. Really. She's a real pickup. She asked me for the price of a cup of tea, and I brought her home with me."

"But what on earth are you going to do with her?" cried Philip.

"Be nice to her," said Rosemary quickly. "Be frightfully nice to her. Look after her. I don't know how. We haven't talked yet. But show her—treat her—make her feel—"

"My darling girl," said Philip, "you're quite mad, you know. It simply can't be done."

"I knew you'd say that," retorted Rosemary. "Why not? I want to. Isn't that a reason? And besides, one's always reading about these things. I decided—"

"But," said Philip slowly, and he cut the end of a cigar, "she's so astonishingly pretty."

"Pretty?" Rosemary was so surprised that she blushed. "Do you think so? I—I hadn't thought about it."

"Good Lord?" Philip struck a match. "She's absolutely lovely. Look again, my child. I was bowled over when I came into your room just now. However...I think you're making a ghastly mistake. Sorry, darling, if I'm crude and all that. But let me know if Miss Smith is going to dine with us in time for me to look up The Milliner's Gazette."

"You absurd creature!" said Rosemary, and she went out of the library, but not back to her bedroom. She went to her writing-room and sat down at her desk. Pretty! Absolutely lovely! Bowled over! Her heart beat like a heavy bell. Pretty! Lovely! She drew her cheque-book towards her. But no, cheques would be no use, of course. She opened a drawer and took out five pound notes, looked at them, put two back, and holding the three squeezed in her hand, she went back to her bedroom.

Half an hour later Philip was still in the library, when Rosemary came in.

"I only wanted to tell you," said she, and she leaned against the door again and looked at him with her dazzled exotic gaze, "Miss

Smith won't dine with us tonight."

Philip put down the paper. "Oh, what's happened? Previous engagement?"

Rosemary came over and sat down on his knee. "She insisted on going," said she, "so I gave the poor little thing a present of money. I couldn't keep her against her will, could I?" she added softly.

Rosemary had just done her hair, darkened her eyes a little, and put on her pearls. She put up her hands and touched Philip's cheeks.

"Do you like me?" said she, and her tone, sweet, husky, troubled him.

"I like you awfully," he said, and he held her tighter. "Kiss me."

There was a pause.

Then Rosemary said dreamily: "I saw a fascinating little box today. It cost twenty-eight guineas. May I have it?"

Philip jumped her on his knee. "You may, little wasteful one," said he.

But that was not really what Rosemary wanted to say.

"Philip," she whispered, and she pressed his head against her bosom, "am I pretty?"

BLISS

Although Bertha Young was thirty she still had moments like this when she wanted to run instead of walk, to take dancing steps on and off the pavement, to bowl a hoop, to throw something up in the air and catch it again, or to stand still and laugh at—nothing—at nothing, simply.

What can you do if you are thirty and, turning the corner of your own street, you are overcome, suddenly, by a feeling of bliss—absolute bliss! —as though you'd suddenly swallowed a bright piece of that late afternoon sun and it burned in your bosom, sending out a little shower of sparks into every particle, into every finger and toe...

Oh, is there no way you can express it without being "drunk and disorderly"? How idiotic civilization is! Why be given a body if you have to keep it shut up in a case like a rare, rare fiddle?

"No, that about the fiddle is not quite what I mean," she thought, running up the steps and feeling in her bag for the key—she'd forgotten it, as usual—and rattling the letter-box. "It's not what I mean, because—Thank you, Mary" —she went into the hall.

"Is nurse back?"

"Yes, M'm."

"And has the fruit come?"

"Yes, M'm. Everything's come."

"Bring the fruit up to the dining-room, will you? I'll arrange it before I go upstairs."

It was dusky in the dining-room and quite chilly. But all the same Bertha threw off her coat; she could not bear the tight clasp of it another moment, and the cold air fell on her arms.

But in her bosom there was still that bright glowing place—that shower of little sparks coming from it. It was almost unbearable. She hardly dared to breathe for fear of fanning it higher, and yet she breathed deeply, deeply. She hardly dared to look into the cold mirror—but she did look, and it gave her back a woman, radiant, with smiling, trembling lips, with big, dark eyes and an air of listening, waiting for something...divine to happen...that she knew must happen...infallibly.

Mary brought in the fruit on a tray and with it a glass bowl, and a blue dish, very lovely, with a strange sheen on it as though it had been dipped in milk.

"Shall I turn on the light, M'm?"

"No, thank you. I can see quite well."

There were tangerines and apples stained with strawberry pink. Some yellow pears, smooth as silk, some white grapes covered with a silver bloom and a big cluster of purple ones. These last she had bought to tone in with the new dining-room carpet. Yes, that did sound rather far-fetched and absurd, but it was really why she had bought them. She had thought in the shop: "I must have some purple ones to bring the carpet up to the table." And it had seemed quite sense at the time.

When she had finished with them and had made two pyramids of these bright round shapes, she stood away from the table to get the effect—and it really was most curious. For the dark table seemed to melt into the dusky light and the glass dish and the blue bowl to float in the air. This, of course in her present mood, was so incredibly beautiful...She began to laugh.

"No, no. I'm getting hysterical." And she seized her bag and coat and ran upstairs to the nursery.

Nurse sat at a low table giving Little B her supper after her bath. The baby had on a white flannel gown and a blue woolen jacket, and her dark, fine hair was brushed up into a funny little peak. She looked up when she saw her mother and began to jump.

"Now, my lovey, eat it up like a good girl," said Nurse, setting her lips in a way that Bertha knew, and that meant she had come into the nursery at another wrong moment.

"Has she been good, Nanny?"

"She's been a little sweet all the afternoon," whispered Nanny. "We went to the park and I sat down on a chair and took her out of the pram and a big dog came along and put its head on my knee and she clutched its ear, tugged it. Oh, you should have seen her."

Bertha wanted to ask if it wasn't rather dangerous to let her clutch at a strange dog's ear. But she did not dare to. She stood watching them, her hands by her side, like the poor little girl in front of the rich little girl with the doll.

The baby looked up at her again, stared, and then smiled so charmingly that Bertha couldn't help crying:

"Oh, Nanny, do let me finish giving her her supper while you put the bath things away."

"Well, M'm, she oughtn't to be changed hands while she's eating," said Nanny, still whispering. "It unsettles her; it's very likely to upset her."

How absurd it was. Why have a baby if it has to be kept—not in a case like a rare, rare fiddle—but in another woman's arms?

"Oh, I must!" said she.

Very offended, Nanny handed her over.

"Now, don't excite her after her supper. You know you do,

M'm. And I have such a time with her after!"

Thank heaven! Nanny went out of the room with the bath towels.

"Now I've got you to myself, my little precious," said Bertha, as the baby leaned against her.

She ate delightfully, holding up her lips for the spoon and then waving her hands. Sometimes she wouldn't let the spoon go; and sometimes, just as Bertha had filled it, she waved it away to the four winds.

When the soup was finished Bertha turned round to the fire.

"You're nice—you're very nice!" said she, kissing her warm baby. "I'm fond of you. I like you."

And, indeed, she loved Little B so much—her neck as she bent forward, her exquisite toes as they shone transparent in the firelight—that all her feeling of bliss came back again, and again she didn't know how to express it—what to do with it.

"You're wanted on the telephone," said Nanny, coming back in triumph and seizing her Little B.

Down she flew. It was Harry.

"Oh, is that you, Ber? Look here. I'll be late. I'll take a taxi and come along as quickly as I can, but get dinner put back ten minutes—will you? All right?"

"Yes, perfectly. Oh, Harry!"

"Yes?"

What had she to say? She'd nothing to say. She only wanted to get in touch with him for a moment. She couldn't absurdly cry: "Hasn't it been a divine day!"

"What is it?" rapped out the little voice.

"Nothing. Entendu," said Bertha, and hung up the receiver, thinking how more than idiotic civilization was.

They had people coming to dinner. The Norman Knights—a very sound couple—he was about to start a theatre, and she was awfully keen on interior decoration, a young man, Eddie Warren, who had just published a little book of poems and whom everybody was asking to dine, and a "find" of Bertha's called Pearl Fulton. What Miss Fulton did, Bertha didn't know. They had met at the club and Bertha had fallen in love with her, as she always did fall in love with beautiful women who had something strange about them.

The provoking thing was that, though they had been about together and met a number of times and really talked, Bertha couldn't yet make her out. Up to a certain point Miss Fulton was rarely, wonderfully frank, but the certain point was there, and beyond that she would not go.

Was there anything beyond it? Harry said "No" .Voted her

dullish, and "cold like all blonde women, with a touch, perhaps, of anaemia of the brain". But Bertha wouldn't agree with him; not yet, at any rate.

"No, the way she has of sitting with her head a little on one side, and smiling, has something behind it, Harry, and I must find out what that something is."

"Most likely it's a good stomach," answered Harry.

He made a point of catching Bertha's heels with replies of that kind..."liver frozen, my dear girl", or "pure flatulence", or "kidney disease"...and so on. For some strange reason Bertha liked this, and almost admired it in him very much.

She went into the drawing-room and lighted the fire; then picking up the cushions, one by one, that Mary had disposed so carefully, she threw them back on to the chairs and the couches. That made all the difference; the room came alive at once. As she was about to throw the last one she surprised herself by suddenly hugging it to her, passionately, passionately. But it did not put out the fire in her bosom. Oh, on the contrary?

The windows of the drawing-room opened on to a balcony overlooking the garden. At the far end, against the wall, there was a tall, slender pear tree in fullest, richest bloom; it stood perfect, as though becalmed against the jade-green sky. Bertha couldn't help feeling, even from this distance, that it had not a single bud or a faded petal. Down below, in the garden beds, the red and yellow tulips, heavy with flowers, seemed to lean upon the dusk. A grey cat, dragging its belly, crept across the lawn, and a black one, its shadow, trailed after. The sight of them, so intent and so quick, gave Bertha a curious shiver.

"What creepy things cats are!" she stammered, and she turned away from the window and began walking up and down...

How strong the jonquils smelled in the warm room. Too strong? Oh, no. And yet, as though overcome, she flung down on a couch and pressed her hands to her eyes.

"I'm too happy—too happy!" she murmured.

And she seemed to see on her eyelids the lovely pear tree with its wide open blossoms as a symbol of her own life.

Really—really—she had everything. She was young. Harry and she were as much in love as ever, and they got on together splendidly and were really good pals. She had an adorable baby. They didn't have to worry about money. They had this absolutely satisfactory house and garden. And friends—modern, thrilling friends, writers and painters and poets or people keen on social questions—just the kind of friends they wanted. And then there were books, and there was music, and she had found a wonderful little dressmaker, and they were going abroad in the summer, and their new cook made the most superb omelettes...

"I'm absurd. Absurd!" She sat up; but she felt quite dizzy, quite drunk. It must have been the spring.

Yes, it was the spring. Now she was so tired she could not drag herself upstairs to dress.

A white dress, a string of jade beads, green shoes and stockings. It wasn't intentional. She had thought of this scheme hours before she stood at the drawing-room window.

Her petals rustled softly into the hall, and she kissed Mrs Norman Knight, who was taking off the most amusing orange coat with a procession of black monkeys round the hem and up the fronts.

"...Why! Why! Why is the middle-class so stodgy—so utterly without a sense of humour! My dear, it's only by a fluke that I am here at all—Norman being the protective fluke. For my darling monkeys so upset the train that it rose to a man and simply ate me with its eyes. Didn't laugh—wasn't amused—that I should have loved. No, just stared—and bored me through and through."

"But the cream of it was," said Norman, pressing a large tortoiseshell-rimmed monocle into his eye, "you don't mind me telling this, Face, do you?" (In their home and among their friends they called each other Face and Mug.) "The cream of it was when she, being full fed, turned to the woman beside her and said: 'Haven't you ever seen a monkey before? ' "

"Oh, yes!" Mrs Norman Knight joined in the laughter. "Wasn't that too absolutely creamy?"

And a funnier thing still was that now her coat was off she did look like a very intelligent monkey—who had even made that yellow silk dress out of scraped banana skins. And her amber earrings, they were like little dangling nuts.

"This is a sad, sad fall!" said Mug, pausing in front of Little B's perambulator. "When the perambulator comes into the hall—" and he waved the rest of the quotation away.

The bell rang. It was lean, pale Eddie Warren (as usual) in a state of acute distress.

"It is the right house, isn't it?" he pleaded.

"Oh, I think so—I hope so," said Bertha brightly.

"I have had such a dreadful experience with a taxi-man; he was most sinister. I couldn't get him to stop. The more I knocked and called the faster he went. And in the moonlight this bizarre figure with the flattened head crouching over the little wheel..."

He shuddered, taking off an immense white silk scarf. Bertha noticed that his socks were white, too—most charming.

"But how dreadful!" she cried.

"Yes, it really was," said Eddie, following her into the drawing-room. "I saw myself driving through Eternity in a timeless taxi."

He knew the Norman Knights. In fact, he was going to write a play for N. K. when the theatre scheme came off.

"Well, Warren, how's the play?" said Norman Knight, dropping his monocle and giving his eye a moment in which to rise to the surface before it was screwed down again.

And Mrs Norman Knight: "Oh, Mr Warren, what happy socks!"

"I am so glad you like them," said he, staring at his feet. "They seem to have got so much whiter since the moon rose." And he turned his lean sorrowful young face to Bertha. "There is a moon, you know."

She wanted to cry: "I am sure there is—often—often!"

He really was a most attractive person. But so was Face, crouched before the fire in her banana skins, and so was Mug, smoking a cigarette and saying as he flicked the ash: "Why doth the bridegroom tarry? "

"There he is, now."

Bang went the front door open and shut. Harry shouted: "Hullo, you people. Down in five minutes." And they heard him swarm up the stairs. Bertha couldn't help smiling; she knew how he loved doing things at high pressure. What, after all, did an extra five minutes matter? But he would pretend to himself that they mattered beyond measure. And then he would make a great point of coming into the drawing-room, extravagantly cool and collected.

Harry had such a zest for life. Oh, how she appreciated it in him. And his passion for fighting—for seeking in everything that came up against him another test of his power and of his courage—that, too, she understood. Even when it made him just occasionally, to other people, who didn't know him well, a little ridiculous perhaps...For there were moments when he rushed into battle where no battle was...She talked and laughed and positively forgot until he had come in (just as she had imagined) that Pearl Fulton had not turned up.

"I wonder if Miss Fulton has forgotten?"

"I expect so," said Harry. "Is she on the phone?"

"Ah! There's a taxi, now." And Bertha smiled with that little air of proprietorship that she always assumed while her women finds were new and mysterious. "She lives in taxis."

"She'll run to fat if she does," said Harry coolly, ringing the bell for dinner. "Frightful danger for blonde women."

"Harry—don't," warned Bertha, laughing up at him.

Came another tiny moment, while they waited, laughing and talking, just a trifle too much at their ease, a trifle too unaware. And then Miss Fulton, all in silver, with a silver fillet binding her pale blonde hair, came in smiling, her head a little on one side.

"Am I late?"

"No, not at all," said Bertha. "Come along." And she took her arm and they moved into the dining-room.

What was there in the touch of that cool arm that could fan—fan—start blazing—blazing—the fire of bliss that Bertha did not know what to do with?

Miss Fulton did not look at her; but then she seldom did look at people directly. Her heavy eyelids lay upon her eyes and the strange half smile came and went upon her lips as though she lived by listening rather than seeing. But Bertha knew, suddenly, as if the longest, most intimate look had passed between them—as if they had said to each other: "You, too?" —that Pearl Fulton, stirring the beautiful red soup in the grey plate, was feeling just what she was feeling.

And the others? Face and Mug, Eddie and Harry, their spoons rising and falling—dabbing their lips with their napkins, crumbling bread, fiddling with the forks and glasses and talking.

"I met her at the Alpha show—the weirdest little person. She'd not only cut off her hair, but she seemed to have taken a dreadfully good snip off her legs and arms and her neck and her poor little nose as well."

"Isn't she very liée with Michael Oat?"

"The man who wrote *Love in False Teeth*?"

"He wants to write a play for me. One act. One man. Decides to commit suicide. Gives all the reasons why he should and why he shouldn't. And just as he has made up his mind either to do it or not to do it—curtain. Not half a bad idea."

"What's he going to call it—'Stomach Trouble'?"

"I think I've come across the same idea in a little French review, quite unknown in England."

No, they didn't share it. They were dears—dears—and she loved having them there, at her table, and giving them delicious food and wine. In fact, she longed to tell them how delightful they were, and what a decorative group they made, how they seemed to set one another off and how they reminded her of a play by Chekhov.

Harry was enjoying his dinner. It was part of his—well, not his nature, exactly, and certainly not his pose—his—something or other—to talk about food and to glory in his "shameless passion for the white flesh of the lobster" and "the green of pistachio ices—green and cold like the eyelids of Egyptian dancers".

When he looked up at her and said: "Bertha, this is a very admirable soufflée!" she almost could have wept with child-like pleasure.

Oh, why did she feel so tender towards the whole world tonight? Everything was good—was right. All that happened seemed to fill again her brimming cup of bliss.

And still, in the back of her mind, there was the pear tree. It would be silver now, in the light of poor dear Eddie's moon, silver as Miss Fulton, who sat there turning a tangerine in her slender fingers that were so pale a light seemed to come from them.

What she simply couldn't make out—what was miraculous—was how she should have guessed Miss Fulton's mood so exactly and so instantly. For she never doubted for a moment that she was right, and yet what had she to go on? Less than nothing.

"I believe this does happen very, very rarely between women. Never between men," thought Bertha. "But while I am making the coffee in the drawing-room perhaps she will 'give a sign'."

What she meant by that she did not know, and what would happen after that she could not imagine.

While she thought like this she saw herself talking and

laughing. She had to talk because of her desire to laugh.

"I must laugh or die."

But when she noticed Face's funny little habit of tucking something down the front of her bodice—as if she kept a tiny, secret hoard of nuts there, too—Bertha had to dig her nails into her hands—so as not to laugh too much.

It was over at last. And: "Come and see my new coffee machine, " said Bertha.

"We only have a new coffee machine once a fortnight," said Harry. Face took her arm this time; Miss Fulton bent her head and followed after.

The fire had died down in the drawing-room to a red, flickering "nest of baby phoenixes", said Face.

"Don't turn up the light for a moment. It is so lovely." And down she crouched by the fire again. "She was always cold...without her little red flannel jacket, of course," thought Bertha.

At that moment Miss Fulton "gave the sign".

"Have you a garden?" said the cool, sleepy voice.

This was so exquisite on her part that all Bertha could do was to obey. She crossed the room, pulled the curtains apart, and opened those long windows.

"There!" she breathed.

And the two women stood side by side looking at the slender, flowering tree. Although it was so still it seemed, like the flame of a candle, to stretch up, to point, to quiver in the bright air, to grow taller as they gazed—almost to touch the rim of the round, silver moon.

How long did they stand there? Both, as it were, caught in that circle of unearthly light, understanding each other perfectly, creatures of another world, and wondering what they were to do in this one with all this blissful treasure that burned in their bosoms and dropped, in silver flowers, from their hair and hands?

Forever—for a moment? And did Miss Fulton murmur: "Yes. Just that." Or did Bertha dream it?

Then the light was snapped on and Face made the coffee and Harry said: "My dear Mrs Knight, don't ask me about my baby. I never see her. I shan't feel the slightest interest in her until she has a lover," and Mug took his eye out of the conservatory for a moment and then put it under glass again and Eddie Warren drank his coffee and set down the cup with a face of anguish as though he had drunk and seen the spider.

"What I want to do is to give the young men a show. I believe London is simply teeming with first-chop, unwritten plays. What I want to say to 'em is: 'Here's the theatre. Fire ahead.'"

"You know, my dear, I am going to decorate a room for the Jacob Nathans. Oh, I am so tempted to do a fried-fish scheme, with the backs of the chairs shaped like frying pans and lovely chip potatoes embroidered all over the curtains."

"The trouble with our young writing men is that they are still too romantic. You can't put out to sea without being seasick and wanting a basin. Well, why won't they have the courage of those basins?"

"A dreadful poem about a girl who was violated by a beggar without a nose in a little wood..."

Miss Fulton sank into the lowest, deepest chair and Harry handed round the cigarettes.

From the way he stood in front of her shaking the silver box and saying abruptly: "Egyptian? Turkish? Virginian? They're all mixed up," Bertha realized that she not only bored him, he really disliked her. And she decided from the way Miss Fulton said: "No, thank you, I won't smoke," that she felt it, too, and was hurt.

"Oh, Harry, don't dislike her. You are quite wrong about her. She's wonderful, wonderful. And, besides, how can you feel so differently about someone who means so much to me. I shall try to tell you when we are in bed tonight what has been happening. What she and I have shared."

At those last words something strange and almost terrifying darted into Bertha's mind. And this something blind and smiling whispered to her: "Soon these people will go. The house will be quiet—quiet. The lights will be out. And you and he will be alone together in the dark room—the warm bed..."

She jumped from her chair and ran over to the piano.

"What a pity someone does not play!" she cried. "What a pity somebody does not play."

For the first time in her life Bertha Young desired her husband.

Oh, she'd loved him—she'd been in love with him, of course, in every other way, but just not in that way. And, equally, of course, she'd understood that he was different. They'd discussed it so often. It had worried her dreadfully at first to find that she was so cold, but after a time it had not seemed to matter. They were so frank with each other—such good pals. That was the best of being modern.

But now—ardently! Ardently! The word ached in her ardent body! Was this what that feeling of bliss had been leading up to? But then—

"My dear," said Mrs Norman Knight, "you know our shame. We are victims of time and train. We live in Hampstead. It's been so nice."

"I'll come with you into the hall," said Bertha. "I loved having you. But you must not miss the last train. That's so awful, isn't it?"

"Have a whisky, Knight, before you go?" called Harry.

"No thanks, old chap."

Bertha squeezed his hand for that as she shook it.

"Good night, good-bye," she cried from the top step, feeling that this self of hers was taking leave of them forever.

When she got back into the drawing-room the others were on the move.

"... Then you can come part of the way in my taxi."

"I shall be so thankful not to have to face another drive alone after my dreadful experience."

"You can get a taxi at the rank just at the end of the street. You won't have to walk more than a few yards."

"That's a comfort. I'll go and put on my coat."

Miss Fulton moved towards the hall and Bertha was following when Harry almost pushed past.

"Let me help you."

Bertha knew that he was repenting his rudeness—she let him go. What a boy he was in some ways—so impulsive—so—simple.

And Eddie and she were left by the fire.

"I wonder if you have seen Bilks' new poem called Table d' Hôte," said Eddie softly. "It's so wonderful. In the last anthology. Have you got a copy? I'd so like to show it to you. It begins with an incredibly beautiful line: 'Why must it always be tomato soup?'"

"Yes," said Bertha. And she moved noiselessly to a table opposite the drawing-room door and Eddie glided noiselessly after her. She picked up the little book and gave it to him; they had not made a sound.

While he looked it up she turned her head towards the hall. And she saw...Harry with Miss Fulton's coat in his arms and Miss Fulton with her back turned to him and her head bent. He tossed the coat away, put his hands on her shoulders, and turned her violently to him. His lips said: "I adore you," and Miss Fulton laid her moonbeam fingers on his cheeks and smiled her sleepy smile. Harry's nostrils quivered; his lips curled back in a hideous grin while he whispered: "Tomorrow," and with her eyelids Miss Fulton said: "Yes."

"Here it is," said Eddie. "Why must it always be tomato soup?" It's so deeply true, don't you feel? Tomato soup is so dreadfully eternal."

"If you prefer," said Harry's voice, very loud, from the hall, "I can phone you a cab to come to the door."

214

"Oh, no. It's not necessary," said Miss Fulton, and she came up to Bertha and gave her the slender fingers to hold.

"Good-bye. Thank you so much."

"Good-bye," said Bertha.

Miss Fulton held her hand a moment longer.

"Your lovely pear tree!" she murmured.

And then she was gone, with Eddie following, like the black cat following the grey cat.

"I'll shut up shop," said Harry, extravagantly cool and collected.

"Your lovely pear tree—pear tree—pear tree!"

Bertha simply ran over to the long windows.

"Oh, what is going to happen now?" she cried.

But the pear tree was as lovely as ever and as full of flower and as still.

AN IDEAL FAMILY

That evening for the first time in his life, as he pressed through the swing door and descended the three broad steps to the pavement, old Mr Neave felt he was too old for the spring. Spring—warm, eager, restless—was there, waiting for him in the golden light, ready in front of everybody to run up, to blow in his white beard, to drag sweetly on his arm. And he couldn't meet her, no; he couldn't square up once more and stride off, jaunty as a young man. He was tired and, although the late sun was still shining, curiously cold, with a numbed feeling all over. Quite suddenly he hadn't the energy, he hadn't the heart to stand this gaiety and bright movement any longer; it confused him. He wanted to stand still, to wave it away with his stick, to say, "Be off with you!" Suddenly it was a terrible effort to greet as usual—tipping his wide-awake with his stick—all the people whom he knew, the friends, acquaintances, shop-keepers, postmen, drivers. But the gay glance that went with the gesture, the kindly twinkle that seemed to say, "I'm a match and more for any of you" —that old Mr Neave could not manage at all. He stumped along, lifting his knees high as if he were walking through air that had somehow grown heavy and solid like water. And the homeward-going crowd hurried by, the trams clanked, the light carts clattered, the big swinging cabs bowled along with that reckless, defiant indifference that one knows only in dreams...

It had been a day like other days at the office. Nothing special had happened. Harold hadn't come back from lunch until close on four. Where had he been? What had he been up to? He wasn't going to let his father know. Old Mr Neave had happened to be in the vestibule, saying good-bye to a caller, when Harold sauntered in, perfectly turned out as usual, cool, suave, smiling that peculiar little half-smile that women found so fascinating.

Ah, Harold was too handsome, too handsome by far; that had been the trouble all along. No man had a right to such eyes, such lashes and such lips; it was uncanny. As for his mother, his sisters, and the servants, it was not too much to say they made a young god of him; they worshipped Harold, they forgave him everything; and he had needed some forgiving ever since the time when he was thirteen and he had stolen his mother's purse, taken the money, and hidden the purse in the cook's bedroom. Old Mr Neave struck sharply with his stick upon the pavement edge. But it wasn't only his family who spoiled Harold, he reflected, it was everybody; he had only to look and to smile, and down they went before him. So perhaps it wasn't to be wondered at that he expected the office to carry on the tradition. H'm, h'm? But it couldn't be done. No business—not even a successful, established, big paying concern—could be played with. A man had either to put his whole heart and soul into it, or it went all to pieces before his eyes...

And then Charlotte and the girls were always at him to make the whole thing over to Harold, to retire, and to spend his time enjoying himself. Enjoying himself! Old Mr Neave stopped dead under a group of ancient cabbage palms outside the Government buildings! Enjoying himself! The wind of evening shook the dark leaves to a thin airy cackle. Sitting at home, twiddling his thumbs, conscious all the while that his life's work was slipping away, dissolving, disappearing through Harold's fine fingers, while Harold smiled...

"Why will you be so unreasonable, father? There's absolutely no need for you to go to the office. It only makes it very awkward for us when people persist in saying how tired you're looking. Here's this huge house and garden. Surely you could be happy in—in—appreciating it for a change. Or you could take up some hobby."

And Lola the baby had chimed in loftily, "All men ought to have hobbies. It makes life impossible if they haven't."

Well, well! He couldn't help a grim smile as painfully he began to climb the hill that led into Harcourt Avenue. Where would Lola and her sisters and Charlotte be if he'd gone in for hobbies, he'd like to know?

Hobbies couldn't pay for the town house and the seaside bungalow, and their horses, and their golf, and the sixty-guinea gramophone in the music-room for them to dance to. Not that he grudged them these things. No, they were smart, good-looking girls, and Charlotte was a remarkable woman; it was natural for them to be in the swim. As a matter of fact, no other house in the town was as popular as theirs; no other family entertained so much. And how many times old Mr Neave, pushing the cigar box across the smoking-room table, had listened to praises of his wife, his girls, of himself even.

"You're an ideal family, sir, an ideal family. It's like something one reads about or sees on the stage."

"That's all right, my boy," old Mr Neave would reply. "Try one of those; I think you'll like them. And if you care to smoke in the garden, you'll find the girls on the lawn, I dare say."

That was why the girls had never married, so people said. They could have married anybody. But they had too good a time at home. They were too happy together, the girls and Charlotte. H'm, h'm! Well, well! Perhaps so...

By this time he had walked the length of fashionable Harcourt Avenue; he had reached the corner house, their house. The carriage gates were pushed back; there were fresh marks of wheels on the drive. And then he faced the big white-painted house, with its wide-open windows, its tulle curtains floating outwards, its blue jars of hyacinths on the broad sills. On either side of the carriage porch their hydrangeas—famous in the town—were coming into flower; the pinkish, bluish masses of flower lay like light among the spreading leaves. And somehow, it seemed to old Mr Neave that the house and the flowers, and even the fresh marks on the drive, were saying, "There is young life here. There are girls—"

The hall, as always, was dusky with wraps, parasols, gloves, piled on the oak chests. From the music-room sounded the piano, quick, loud and impatient. Through the drawing-room door that was ajar voices floated.

"And were there ices?" came from Charlotte. Then the creak, creak of her rocker.

"Ices!" cried Ethel. "My dear mother you never saw such ices. Only two kinds. And one a common little strawberry shop ice, in a sopping wet frill."

"The food altogether was too appalling," came from Marion.

"Still, it's rather early for ices," said Charlotte easily.

"But why, if one has them at all..." began Ethel.

"Oh, quite so, darling," crooned Charlotte.

Suddenly the music-room door opened and Lola dashed out. She started, she nearly screamed, at the sight of old Mr Neave.

"Gracious, father! What a fright you gave me! Have you just come home? Why isn't Charles here to help you off with your coat?"

Her cheeks were crimson from playing, her eyes glittered, and the hair fell over her forehead. And she breathed as though she had come running through the dark and was frightened. Old Mr Neave stared at his youngest daughter; he felt he had never seen her before. So that was Lola, was it? But she seemed to have forgotten her father; it was not for him that she was waiting there. Now she put the tip of her crumpled handkerchief between her teeth and tugged at it angrily. The telephone rang. A-ah! Lola gave a cry like a sob and dashed past him. The door of the telephone-room slammed, and at the same moment Charlotte called, "Is that you, father?"

"You're tired again," said Charlotte reproachfully, and she stopped the rocker and offered him her warm plum-like cheek. Bright-haired Ethel pecked his beard; Marion's lips brushed his ear.

"Did you walk back, father?" asked Charlotte.

"Yes, I walked home," said old Mr Neave, and he sank into one of the immense drawing-room chairs.

"But why didn't you take a cab?" said Ethel. "There are hundreds of cabs about at that time."

"My dear Ethel," cried Marion, "if father prefers to tire himself out, I really don't see what business of ours it is to interfere."

"Children, children!" coaxed Charlotte.

But Marion wouldn't be stopped. "No, mother, you spoil father, and it's not right. You ought to be stricter with him. He's very naughty." She laughed her hard, bright laugh and patted her hair in a mirror. Strange! When she was a little girl she had such a soft, hesitating voice; she had even stuttered, and now, whatever she said—even if it was only "Jam, please, father"—it rang out as though she were on the stage.

"Did Harold leave the office before you, dear?" asked Charlotte, beginning to rock again.

"I'm not sure," said old Mr Neave.

"I'm not sure. I didn't see him after four o'clock."

"He said—" began Charlotte.

But at that moment Ethel, who was twitching over the leaves of some paper or other, ran to her mother and sank down beside her chair.

"There, you see," she cried. "That's what I mean, mummy. Yellow, with touches of silver. Don't you agree?"

"Give it to me, love," said Charlotte. She fumbled for her tortoise-shell spectacles and put them on, gave the page a little dab with her plump small fingers, and pursed up her lips. "Very sweet!" she crooned vaguely; she looked at Ethel over her spectacles. "But I shouldn't have the train."

"Not the train!" wailed Ethel tragically. "But the train's the whole point."

"Here, mother, let me decide." Marion snatched the paper playfully from Charlotte. "I agree with mother," she cried triumphantly. "The train overweights it."

Old Mr Neave, forgotten, sank into the broad lap of his chair, and, dozing, heard them as though he dreamed. There was no doubt about it, he was tired out; he had lost his hold. Even Charlotte and the girls were too much for him tonight. They were too...too...But all his drowsing brain could think of was—too rich for him. And somewhere at the back of everything he was watching a little withered ancient man climbing up endless flights of stairs. Who was he?

"I shan't dress tonight," he muttered.

"What do you say, father?"

"Eh, what, what?" Old Mr Neave woke with a start and stared across at them. "I shan't dress tonight," he repeated.

"But, father, we've got Lucile coming, and Henry Davenport, and Mrs Teddie Walker."

"It will look so very out of the picture."

"Don't you feel well, dear?"

"You needn't make any effort. What is Charles for?"

"But if you're really not up to it," Charlotte wavered.

"Very well! Very well!" Old Mr Neave got up and went to join that little old climbing fellow just as far as his dressing-room...

There young Charles was waiting for him. Carefully, as though everything depended on it, he was tucking a towel round the hot-water can. Young Charles had been a favourite of his ever since as a little red-faced boy he had come into the house to look after the fires. Old Mr Neave lowered himself into the cane lounge by the window, stretched out his legs, and made his little evening joke, "Dress him up, Charles!" And Charles, breathing intensely and frowning, bent forward to take the pin out of his tie.

H'm, h'm! Well, well! It was pleasant by the open window, very pleasant—a fine mild evening. They were cutting the grass on the tennis court below; he heard the soft churr of the mower. Soon the girls would begin their tennis parties again. And at the thought he seemed to hear Marion's voice ring out, "Good for you, partner...Oh, played, partner....Oh, very nice indeed." Then Charlotte calling from the veranda, "Where is Harold?" And Ethel, "He's certainly not here, mother." And Charlotte's vague, "He said—"

Old Mr Neave sighed, got up, and putting one hand under his beard, he took the comb from young Charles, and carefully combed the white beard over. Charles gave him a folded handkerchief, his watch and seals, and spectacle case.

"That will do, my lad." The door shut, he sank back, he was alone...

And now that little ancient fellow was climbing down endless flights that led to a glittering, gay dining-room. What legs he had? They were like a spider's—thin, withered.

"You're an ideal family, sir, an ideal family."

But if that were true, why didn't Charlotte or the girls stop him? Why was he all alone, climbing up and down? Where was Harold? Ah, it was no good expecting anything from Harold. Down, down went the little old spider, and then, to his horror, old Mr Neave saw him slip past the dining-room and make for the porch, the dark drive, the carriage gates, the office. Stop him, stop him, somebody!

Old Mr Neave started up. It was dark in his dressing-room; the window shone pale. How long had he been asleep? He listened, and through the big, airy, darkened house there floated far-away voices, far-away sounds. Perhaps, he thought vaguely, he had been asleep for a long time. He'd been forgotten. What had all this to do with him—this house and Charlotte, the girls and Harold—what did he know about them? They were strangers to him. Life had passed him by. Charlotte was not his wife. His wife!

...A dark porch, half hidden by a passion-vine, which drooped sorrowful, mournful, as though it understood. Small, warm arms were round his neck. A face, little and pale, lifted to his, and a voice breathed, "Good-bye, my treasure."

My treasure! "Good-bye, my treasure!" Which of them had spoken? Why had they said good-bye? There had been some terrible mistake. She was his wife, that little pale girl, and all the rest of his life had been a dream.

Then the door opened, and young Charles, standing in the light, put his hands by his side and shouted like a young soldier, "Dinner is on the table, sir!"

"I'm coming, I'm coming," said old Mr Neave.

THE WIND BLOWS

Suddenly—dreadfully—she wakes up. What has happened? Something dreadful has happened. No—nothing has happened. It is only the wind shaking the house, rattling the windows, banging a piece of iron on the roof and making her bed tremble. Leaves flutter past the window, up and away; down in the avenue a whole newspaper wags in the air like a lost kite and falls, spiked on a pine tree. It is cold. Summer is over—it is autumn—everything is ugly. The carts rattle by, swinging from side to side; two Chinamen lollop along under their wooden yokes with the straining vegetable baskets—their pigtails and blue blouses fly out in the wind. A white dog on three legs yelps past the gate. It is all over! What is? Oh, everything! And she begins to plait her hair with shaking fingers, not daring to look in the glass. Mother is talking to grandmother in the hall.

"A perfect idiot! Imagine leaving anything out on the line in weather like this...Now my best little teneriffe-work tea cloth is simply in ribbons. What is that extraordinary smell? It's the porridge burning. Oh, heavens—this wind!"

She has a music lesson at ten o'clock. At the thought the minor movement of the Beethoven begins to play in her head, the trills long and terrible like little rolling drums...Marie Swainson runs into the garden next door to pick the "chrysanthemums" before they are ruined. Her skirt flies up above her waist; she tries to beat it down, to tuck it between her legs while she stoops, but it is no use—up it flies. All the trees and bushes beat about her. She picks as quickly as she can, but she is quite distracted. She doesn't mind what she does—she pulls the plants up by the roots and bends and twists them, stamping her foot and swearing.

"For heaven's sake keep the front door shut! Go round to the back," shouts someone. And then she hears Bogey:

"Mother, you're wanted on the telephone. Telephone, Mother. It's the butcher."

How hideous life is—revolting, simply revolting...And now her hat-elastic's snapped. Of course it would. She'll wear her old tam and slip out the back way. But Mother has seen.

"Matilda. Matilda. Come back im-me-diately! What on earth have you got on your head? It looks like a tea cosy. And why have you got that mane of hair on your forehead."

"I can't come back, Mother. I'll be late for my lesson."

"Come back immediately!"

She won't. She won't. She hates Mother. "Go to hell," she shouts, running down the road.

In waves, in clouds, in big round whirls the dust comes stinging, and with it little bits of straw and chaff and manure. There is a loud roaring sound from the trees in the gardens, and standing at the bottom of the road outside Mr Bullen's gate she can hear the sea sob: "Ah!...Ah!...Ah-h!" But Mr Bullen's drawing-room is as quiet as a cave. The windows are closed, the blinds half-pulled, and she is not late. The-girl-before-her has just started playing Mac-Dowell's "To an Iceberg". Mr Bullen looks over at her and half smiles.

"Sit down," he says. "Sit over there in the sofa corner, little lady."

How funny he is. He doesn't exactly laugh at you...but there is just something...Oh, how peaceful it is here. She likes this room. It smells of art serge and stale smoke and chrysanthemums... there is a big vase of them on the mantelpiece behind the pale photograph of Rubinstein...à *mon ami Robert Bullen*... Over the black glittering piano hangs "Solitude"—a dark tragic woman draped in white, sitting on a rock, her knees crossed, her chin on her hands.

"No, no!" says Mr Bullen, and he leans over the other girl, puts his arms over her shoulders and plays the passage for her. The stupid—she's blushing? How ridiculous?

Now the-girl-before-her has gone; the front door slams. Mr Bullen comes back and walks up and down, very softly, waiting for her. What an extraordinary thing. Her fingers tremble so that she can't undo the knot in the music satchel. It's the wind...And her heart beats so hard she feels it must lift her blouse up and down. Mr Bullen does not say a word. The shabby red piano seat is long enough for two people to sit side by side. Mr Bullen sits down by her.

"Shall I begin with scales?" she asks, squeezing her hands together. "I had some arpeggios, too."

But he does not answer. She doesn't believe he even hears...and then suddenly his fresh hand with the ring on it reaches over and opens Beethoven.

"Let's have a little of the old master," he says.

But why does he speak so kindly—so awfully kindly—and as though they had known each other for years and years and knew everything about each other.

He turns the page slowly. She watches his hand—it is a very nice hand and always looks as though it had just been washed.

"Here we are," says Mr Bullen.

Oh, that kind voice—Oh, that minor movement. Here come the little drums...

"Shall I take the repeat?"

"Yes, dear child."

His voice is far, far too kind. The crotchets and quavers are dancing up and down the stave like little black boys on a fence.

Why is he so...She will not cry—she has nothing to cry about...

"What is it, dear child?"

Mr Bullen takes her hands. His shoulder is there—just by her head. She leans on it ever so little, her cheek against the springy tweed.

"Life is so dreadful," she murmurs, but she does not feel it's dreadful at all. He says something about "waiting" and "marking time" and "that rare thing, a woman", but she does not hear. It is so comfortable... forever...

Suddenly the door opens and in pops Marie Swainson, hours before her time.

"Take the allegretto a little faster," says Mr Bullen, and gets up and begins to walk up and down again.

"Sit in the sofa corner, little lady," he says to Marie.

The wind, the wind. It's frightening to be here in her room by herself. The bed, the mirror, the white jug and basin gleam like the sky outside. It's the bed that is frightening. There it lies, sound asleep...Does Mother imagine for one moment that she is going to darn all those stockings knotted up on the quilt like a coil of snakes? She's not. No, Mother. I do not see why I should...The wind—the wind! There's a funny smell of soot blowing down the chimney. Hasn't anyone written poems to the wind? ... "I bring fresh flowers to the leaves and showers."...What nonsense.

"Is that you, Bogey?"

"Come for a walk round the esplanade, Matilda. I can't stand this any longer."

"Right-o. I'll put on my ulster. Isn't it an awful day?" Bogey's ulster is just like hers. Hooking the collar she looks at herself in the glass. Her face is white, they have the same excited eyes and hot lips. Ah, they know those two in the glass—Good-bye, dears; we shall be back soon.

"This is better, isn't it?"

"Hook on," says Bogey.

They cannot walk fast enough. Their heads bent, their legs just touching, they stride like one eager person through the town, down the asphalt zigzag where the fennel grows wild, and on to the esplanade. It is dusky—just getting dusky. The wind is so strong that they have to fight their way through it, rocking like two old drunkards. All the poor little pohutukawas on the esplanade are bent to the ground.

"Come on? Come on? Let's get near."

Over by the breakwater the sea is very high. They pull off their hats and her hair blows across her mouth, tasting of salt. The sea is so high that the waves do not break at all; they thump against the rough stone wall and suck up the weedy, dripping steps. A fine spray skims from the water right across the esplanade. They are covered with drops; the inside of her mouth tastes wet and cold.

Bogey's voice is breaking. When he speaks he rushes up and down the scale. It's funny—it makes you laugh—and yet it just suits the day. The wind carries their voices—away fly the sentences like narrow ribbons.

"Quicker! Quicker?"

It is getting very dark. In the harbour the coal hulks show two lights—one high on a mast, and one from the stern.

"Look, Bogey. Look over there."

A big black steamer with a long loop of smoke streaming, with the portholes lighted, with lights everywhere, is putting out to sea. The wind does not stop her; she cuts through the waves, making for the open gate between the pointed rocks that leads to... It's the light that makes her look so awfully beautiful and mysterious...They are on board leaning over the rail arm in arm.

"...Who are they?"

"...Brother and sister."

"Look, Bogey, there's the town. Doesn't it look small? There's the post office clock chiming for the last time. There's the esplanade where we walked that windy day. Do you remember? I cried at my music lesson that day—how many years ago! Good-bye, little island, good-bye..."

Now the dark stretches a wing over the tumbling water. They can't see those two anymore. Good-bye, good-bye. Don't forget...But the ship is gone, now.

The wind—the wind.